UNDERCOVER BILLIONAIRE

MELANIE KNIGHT

WINDYHOPE STAR PRESS

For Danny, Jordene, Ayla, Zev, Hailey, Aidan and Connor. So many wonderful memories, and so many more to come. All my love.

CHAPTER 1

"*And*, that, ladies and gentlemen, is why I shall be victorious."

From any other man, the statement would have been boastful, exaggerated or most likely both, a product of over-confidence, arrogance and a distinct dearth of modesty. Yet his confidence was warranted, the arrogance, though present, was tolerated, and no complaint given for the lack of modesty.

For it was simply true.

Cameron Drake was a man who achieved his goals. He wielded power like a warrior, wrapped in a tycoon's golden thread, his hair a rich auburn, his emerald eyes shimmering with fierce intelligence. His face was chiseled perfection, curves and angles masterfully formed, with full sensual lips and high cheekbones. He rose inches over six feet, with a heavily muscled body no Armani suit could disguise.

Yet far more than physical features made this man the center of attention, as he gazed at a courtroom filled with million-dollar lawyers, powerful politicians and a corporate defendant who saw no reason not to dump toxic waste in a freshwater lake. The defendant was spending millions to keep doing it.

Cameron was not going to let that happen.

He represented a group of people, who joined together to fight the international juggernaut that would destroy pristine lakes, home and hearth to an aquatic wonderland. They couldn't afford a law firm like the one he owned, in which millions exchanged hands, yet for this case, it didn't matter. He had billions, which meant he could defend the causes he believed in – pro bono.

Cameron stood still, seconds after the closing arguments, commanding the courtroom like Poseidon ruled the sea. The jury watched silently, portraits of emotion from his riveting speech, as his clients beamed in delighted disbelief, their confidence evidenced by watery eyes. And the defendants? Their horrified expressions revealed their destruction was over.

Indeed, this man always got what he wanted.

Yet despite collecting legal wins like a child gathers trading cards, Cameron had been restless recently. Something seemed missing – something or *someone*. For most people, this restlessness would have elicited a tangle of hopelessness, frustration or despair, yet challenges only invigorated him. It focused him on the hunt, propelled him to victory. Whatever would cure the restlessness, he would find it.

"MOIST CHOCOLATE FUDGE brownie covered in raspberry ganache."

A soft sigh, a turning page.

"Strawberry shortcake with freshly whipped cream."

Another page, and this time a gasp.

"Whoa. Rocky Road, Dulce de Leche and Chocolate Chip

Cookie Dough ice cream, smothered in hot fudge, dripping in gooey caramel and covered with glitter sprinkles and three cherries. Strike that, the entire bottle of cherries."

Kaitlyn Owens tiptoed through the room, edging towards the woman whose nose actually touched the tablet. The photograph showed an iconic surfer with golden blond hair and simpering blue eyes, gazing into the camera with come-hither adoration. Kaitlyn stopped directly behind the woman. "I'd say Special Value Instant Oatmeal, the banana – no, the prune – type."

Kaitlyn grinned as Allison, her closest and oldest friend, jumped and pivoted, flushing at being caught indulging in one succulent sundae. Standing in the backroom of *The Candy Cane Bakery and Confectionary*, the woman was supposed to be helping in the honest work of chocolate and pastry production, but instead of toiling in the trenches of flour and sugar, she had been distracted by hot buns of a different type.

Yet the guilt quickly transformed into disbelief. "Are you nuts? Just look at him, at all of them! They're perfect..."

Had she missed something? Kaitlyn commandeered the tablet, flipping through the pages of so-called delicacies. They were a cornucopia of romance novel heroes, from blond movie stars to tall, dark and handsome princes – chiseled, defined and heavily muscled. Her answer was obvious. "Yup, definitely prune instant oatmeal."

Her friend sighed, as if she knew further argument would be fruitless and simply hadn't the strength to try. "All right," she conceded, abandoning her precious gossip website and striding to the worktable. "So my dream man and his friends are instant oatmeal." At Kaitlyn's pointed look, she elaborated, "The prune type. Then who could possibly rank ice cream sundae in the opinion of picky Miss Owens?"

Kaitlyn joined her friend on the bench and gazed at the

small chamber filled to the brim with candy-making equipment and supplies. Rainbow walls and glittering floors accentuated silver racks, laden with whimsical cakes and pastries. The air was fresh and sweet, scented with fresh chocolate chip cookies and vanilla cake. This was her dream come true, a sweet Florida candy and pastry store built with hard work and dedication. After years of toiling, the small shop finally turned a profit, and business was booming. Best of all, she earned enough to give back to the community through free workshops and donations to those in need.

"First let me say I do not need or desire a man, but if I did..." A vision formed, the easy-going man who would fit perfectly into her hectic life. "He would be average sized, probably not very big or muscular. He doesn't have to be the greatest looking of men, but nice and modest. Quiet and shy, yet considerate and good. He would listen to me. He would be very agreeable and sort of... what's the word? Mellow. Yes, mellow."

"That's your perfect 10?" Allison gaped. "Are you certain you're not talking about a puppy?"

Kaitlyn laughed. She attracted her fair share of men, yet the type of male who pursued her left much to be desired. Her last three boyfriends, Mr. Wrong, Mr. Really Wrong and Mr. I-Thought-Neanderthals-Were-Extinct Wrong, proved that. Big and burly, aggressive and narcissistic, the men were more interested in a trophy girlfriend than in a true woman or relationship. If she ever had time to date, she would choose a non-aggressive gentleman who would let her be who and what she wanted. "Sounds perfect to me." Kaitlyn grabbed a handful of gooey cookie dough and began to shape miniature hearts. "But it doesn't matter anyway. Like I said, I don't need a man."

"Mail call!"

Kaitlyn smiled as the letter carrier, an elderly man with

soft laugh lines etched on his kindly face, placed a thick pile on the side bench. "Good morning, Frank. How are you?"

"Wonderful." Aged eyes sparkled with mirth. "Thank you again for the surprise gift basket for the wife. It cheered her right up after the surgery."

"Of course." She smiled warmly. "On your way out, stop by the counter. I have a little something for both of you."

His ruddy cheeks deepened. "You don't have to spoil us."

Perhaps not, but it felt great.

She palmed another handful of sticky batter, halted as an unobtrusive letter peeked out from under the stack. She placed down the batter, wiped her hands on her apron and reached for the small brown envelope.

Her heart stuttered as she uncovered the return address. She clutched the envelope tighter, crinkling it in pale fingers, before swiftly tearing it open, accidently ripping the folded note within. The scent of cheap perfume tickled her nose as she brought out a thin piece of paper with three single sentences:

I'm taking you up on your standing offer. See you Friday for a week visit. I can't wait to meet your better half. Cynthia

She read the contents of the missive. Then she read it again. She read it once more. And yet its contents remained the same, the modern version of a gauntlet thrown from across the country.

"What is it?" Allison asked in a low voice. All signs of mirth had vanished, in a charged atmosphere that couldn't be missed. "Has something happened?"

Kaitlyn folded the offending letter and placed it into the envelope. She picked up the batter for the next heart, moving in methodical motions, as the letter repeated itself in her mind. She made a dozen hearts before her hands stilled on the mushy batter. She let out a deep, low breath. "I never thought it would come to this," she whispered.

Allison brought her hands to her lips, her expression tinted with dread. "What is it?"

Then Kaitlyn uttered the most tragic words ever voiced in human existence:

"I need a man."

Allison stood silent, too shocked to speak. Kaitlyn breathed deeply. Her friend clearly appreciated the grave implications of the statement. Caught in a position of vulnerability and the need for... a man. The situation deserved a moment of silence.

"I'm sorry." Allison shook her head. "I thought you said..."

"I need a man," Kaitlyn repeated miserably. "I don't believe it."

"Neither do I. But backtrack for a second." Alison pointed to the folded paper. "I'm assuming your announcement has to do with that letter."

"Unfortunately." Kaitlyn picked up the discarded piece of mail, keeping it at arm's length as if a rabid dog poised to bite. "My cousin Cynthia has decided to visit. In just a few days she will invade my home, where she will expect my boyfriend and I to welcome her."

"Boyfriend?" Allison opened her mouth, closed it. "You have a boyfriend?"

"No. Yes. No." Kaitlyn rubbed the bridge of her nose, where a dull ache had started to throb. Her cousin hadn't yet arrived and already she was upending her life. "As children, Cynthia deemed it her mission to best me in any and every way possible. It is a practice she's carried into adulthood."

"Sounds like she never made it past her teens."

"Precisely. Every so often she calls to gloat about this or that, always in a sugar-coated manner that rubs me like fingernails on a chalkboard. A couple of years ago, she spent an hour bragging about her wonderful boyfriend and ridiculing my lack thereof. I finally had enough. I concocted a story about a fictional boyfriend and enjoyed a splendid afternoon convincing her I scored the greatest man of the season."

She shrugged. "I never thought it would matter. How could she ever discover my lie? She's not on social media and doesn't keep in touch with the rest of the family, at least not since the incident at my cousin's wedding, which involved several groomsmen, an extraordinary amount of tequila and not a lot of clothing." She winced. "According to this letter, however, she's coming in three days and is *very* excited to see my fairytale prince. Which is why I have to start kissing every frog in town."

"But it still doesn't make sense." Allison held up her hands. "You go after what you want, and I've never seen you afraid of anyone. Why don't you just tell her the truth?"

"I can't." Kaitlyn breathed out. "I'm not embarrassed or ashamed I don't have a fairytale prince, if he even exists. Like I said before, I don't want or need him, and I'll tell that to a thousand Cynthias. I just don't want her to know I got worked up enough to lie about it. Could you imagine her gloating to every relative from my mother to fifth cousin? She'd end the family feud just to do it!"

Allison frowned. "Couldn't you just tell her you broke up?"

If only it were that easy. "It won't work. Cynthia may be horrible, but she's not stupid. Whenever she asked about him, I said things were going great. I kept meaning to tell her we broke up but then she'd gloat, and it was just easier to maintain the ruse. Unfortunately, she called last week for her annual 'I'm better than you' conversation, and I mentioned him. If I don't produce Mr. Wonderful, she'll assume I lied. Same thing if I tell her she can't come."

Allison looked at the letter. "Why would she even want to come? It doesn't sound like you're best buddies."

"We're not. The standing invitation was given ten years ago! After mentioning some issues with a current boyfriend and a former best friend – three guesses on what happened there – she asked if I was going to be in town for the next few weeks. She knows I have nothing big planned. Things must have gotten complicated, and since she's insulted every other relative, she's using me as free rent until the situation calms." She raked her hand through her hair. "If I can just get through this visit, I promise to invent a quick breakup and never lie again. Yet where am I going to find a prince in just three days?"

A mischievous grin lit Allison's face. "Oh, you don't need actual royalty. You just need someone to play him. And I know exactly where to look."

WHEN ALLISON first suggested finding a man through a brochure, Kaitlyn assumed she'd been joking. Pick a man out of a catalog? It sounded like something from a torrid 90's movie. However, after a thorough explanation, the idea sounded not only feasible but logical. She didn't need a man, she needed one to pretend to be *her* man. Who could do the job better than an actor?

And where could she find an actor on such short notice? To her astonishment, they actually made brochures for that type of thing, and her friend had them. Apparently, Allison, a private investigator, used some of the companies on prior cases, all of which turned out successful. She'd gladly lent Kaitlyn the pamphlets.

Now she sat on the plush jacquard sofa of her brightly lit living room, clutching one of the brochures. Kaitlyn lived on the floor above her store, in a small apartment converted from an unfinished loft. Scented with the delicious aromas of cookies and cakes, it had only a single bedroom and bathroom, but an open floor plan combined with aesthetically placed decorations created an atmosphere that seemed almost spacious. Pine furniture, flowering plants and posters of scenic landscapes created a charming space, perfect for destressing after a long day of candy creating.

Now she was searching for a delicacy of a different type. An actor would be perfect for her situation. She wouldn't have to worry about the calamities of a normal relationship – fighting, break-ups, messy emotions. No risk of an explosive fight or lover's quarrel in front of the ever-watchful Cynthia. And best of all, she could specify exactly the type of man she wanted. No aggressive, self-righteous, full-of-himself man for her. It was the ultimate solution.

Kaitlyn held up the most promising brochure: *The Actors Association*. The rates seemed reasonable, the operation professional. They hailed from Houston, far from the Florida town of Greenfield she called home, but they boasted nationwide coverage. Since they flew someone out, it cost a decent amount – payable upfront – but the success of the shop afforded her a little extra cash. She dialed the number and was immediately connected with a receptionist who confirmed availability and price.

Everything appeared legitimate, and yet still she hesitated. Could she really hire an actor to pretend to be her boyfriend? A picture of Cynthia flashed, and she notched up her chin. "I'm ready to place my order."

In a daze, Kaitlyn answered the receptionist's questions, paid by credit card and reluctantly scheduled the actor for the very next day. Cynthia would arrive Friday night, and it was already Tuesday. Unfortunately, the time to prepare *with* the actor had to take priority over the time to prepare *for* the actor. She refused to compromise on one aspect, however – the type of man she'd be shackled to for Cynthia's visit.

When the clerk asked for performer specifications,

Kaitlyn launched into her speech. "Not too big or aggressive. Mild-mannered, calm and quiet. Maybe not exactly meek, but well, actually meek sounds great. Easy-going with a capital E. Someone who will listen to me and do what is expected without a problem."

She might have to share a fictitious relationship, but it would be with a man she could tolerate. The receptionist assured her they had the perfect performer, who fit her description exactly. He would arrive at 8 o'clock sharp the next evening.

Ignoring the slight feeling of uneasiness that accompanies one's hiring of a stranger to play a loving boyfriend, Kaitlyn agreed to the terms and completed the call.

Tomorrow loomed like a threatening storm. For the first time in years, a man would hover, pretending to be her boyfriend. Would he look at her with come-hither eyes, pepper feather-light touches on her body? Not only must she allow it, but she would encourage it. As she got ready for bed, she couldn't quite quell her worries, strangely more intense over the actor's arrival than that of her cousin. All would be well…

As long as she kept control.

WEDNESDAY MORNING DAWNED in stormy glory. Gray clouds darkened a sunless sky, all traces of cerulean hidden beneath their gloomy depths. Howling winds blew through rickety old trees and over weathered grasses, sending wet leaves scattering through the air. Kaitlyn slept through her alarm, and only the rumbling of thunder finally roused her from slumber.

In minutes, she consumed a morning meal of cereal and toast, then spent half an hour selecting an outfit. She donned a silk cream-colored blouse with a wide scoop neckline and sheer sleeves, which mixed femininity and businesswoman to harmonious perfection. The matching silk skirt fell to just above her knees, ending in a wisp of sheer chiffon. Long enough to be casual, but short enough to show off her legs, the skirt seemingly floated around her. A single diamond solitaire on an elegant golden chain completed the outfit.

She raced down to the store and completed her morning preparations. In addition to all sorts of candy, the store offered a variety of cakes and pastries, baked from the freshest ingredients each day. She passed a fudge supreme cake dripping in chocolate, a strawberry shortcake with homemade whipped cream and chocolate croissants still warm from the oven. Her employees had already started crafting the morning's delicacies, scenting the air with their delicious aroma.

Kaitlyn gave a warm greeting to Lily, her baker, and started setting out the rest of the morning displays. Time passed quickly, and the opening hour soon rolled around. Despite the turbulent weather, the store grew busy, and time whizzed by in a hectic but enjoyable rush. It was not until late afternoon that she finally noticed how bad the storm had become. The once light gray sky loomed as dark as night, setting a horror movie backdrop to the thick raindrops that pelted against the windows, hard enough to shake the sturdy glass. Large balls of hail accompanied the rain, shattering against the sidewalk in deafening crashes like a marching band's drum, only to be drowned out by the incessant rumbling of thunder. Now concerned about her actor's imminent arrival, Kaitlyn left the store in her employees' capable hands and hurried upstairs to call the acting company.

The same receptionist answered the phone and listened as Kaitlyn apprised her of the situation. The clerk knew of the inclement weather and assured her the flight should arrive on time despite the storm. If the actor couldn't make it that night, he would be there early the next morning.

The afternoon passed almost as quickly as the morning, although business was slower for the nastiness outside. At half past seven, Kaitlyn finished the last of her closing procedures and returned to her apartment. Since the actor would provide his own transportation from the airport, she hadn't recorded his airline information. With no way to check if his flight arrived as scheduled, she could do nothing but wait.

Another bolt of thunder raged, and the lights flickered, amidst a disturbing thought. Originally, she planned to house the actor in a hotel a few blocks away, even during her cousin's visit. She would pretend he wanted to give her quality time alone with her cousin, which would reduce the risk of Cynthia uncovering the ruse. If he managed to arrive safely, however, she couldn't possibly send him out again in Greenfield's own virtual hurricane.

Like it or not, she would be sharing the house with a stranger, at least for the night.

She caught sight of the brochure, smiled and relaxed. There was nothing to fear. Her specified man would be no more threatening than a kitten, and probably just as small. Satisfied with logic's reassurance, she curled up on the cozy couch, a romance novel in one hand and a glass of white zinfandel in the other, to await the beckoning of the doorbell.

Eight o'clock arrived with neither the actor's arrival nor a phone call. No problem. She wasn't really, really, really, really grateful for the delay or anything. Even if the plane arrived on time, the performer would likely move slower in the midst of the storm. She waited and waited, putting down the book when she re-read the same scene four times. Nine o'clock arrived, followed swiftly by ten. Fate had granted a reprieve; likely her guest would not arrive until the next day.

She all but did a happy dance. Okay, she actually did perform a happy dance, but it was a small one. Relieved for reasons she wouldn't explore, she reclined on the soft sofa and allowed sleep to overtake her.

"Damn!"

The late model Porsche hydroplaned through the dangerously wet roads, squealing in indignation as the lone driver jerked the steering wheel to the left. A tree appeared out of the darkness, solid and thick and closer and closer and… he veered to the right, swiping as close to the jagged bark as a lover's caress.

Narrowly missing *another* fallen tree, Cameron Drake regained control of the embattled vehicle, exhaling air heavy with the scent of rain and oak, even in the luxurious cabin. Lightning flashed and thunder boomed, heralding his close call, the third almost-catastrophe in as many minutes. Would he emerge intact from the next one?

He drove with restraint, moving as slowly as possible, yet the vicious storm pounded and pummeled the world around him, unforgivable and unrelenting. Like it or not, the elements held Cameron at their mercy tonight. Frustrating and exasperating for a man accustomed to ruling his world.

No sane person would be on the road on such a night, as a virtual hurricane loomed from above. He hadn't even planned to come through the small town, but half the roads on his typical route were impassable, the other half dangerous. How had something so right turned so very wrong?

It had been a good day, a great one even. He won yet another case, awarding the firm that bore his name another win against those who would destroy the environment. He argued the trial in Gainesville, which, difficult as it was to believe, resided relatively close to his current location. After the case, his colleagues took the first flight back to Miami, and although he held a golden ticket with the same destination, he foolishly declined. More work remained to wrap up the logistics of the case. Leave a job unfinished? That was not how he became the overnight star of the legal world.

At thirty-three years of age, Cameron already posed a major player. He'd worked his way up from a modest upbringing to receive a full scholarship to Harvard. From there he progressed to law school, graduating at the top of his class. He had been accepted into a prestigious law firm in Miami, became their prodigy and won case after case. In an unheard-of scarcity of years, Cameron had branched off into his own multibillion-dollar firm. Now the owner and senior partner of *The Drake Association*, he'd finally achieved his goals, and was part of the elite group the press dubbed the *Billionaires of Miami*.

He'd traded his plane ticket for an evening flight, which gave him plenty of time to finish his work. Unfortunately, the elements didn't respect his dedication as much as the legal field and upended his flight. Instead of taking a one-day hiatus from the Association, he decided to drive. How hard could it be? Yet as he swerved around another fallen branch, the answer was clear:

Too hard.

He let out another slow breath, squinting past the rapidly swaying yet hopelessly outmaneuvered windshield wipers. Three droplets replaced every one it felled, leaving a small river flowing above his dash. A thundering gale shook the vehicle, its tendrils reaching a towering oak mere yards ahead. He hit the brakes, skidding as the tree swayed back and forth, one way and then another like a drunk ballroom dancer. The tree shook and crunched, crackled and then....

Snapped.

The world seemingly moved in slow motion, as the

massive tree fell, down, down, down. The car was slowing, but was it enough? With a thunderous boom, the tree crashed into the ground.... just missing him.

Cameron eased his foot back onto the accelerator. He had to find shelter, and he had to find it now. Even a stranger's house couldn't be more dangerous than nature's fury. Of course, his third degree black belt could help just in case he picked the one mass murderer on the road. As if by fate's mercy, a light sparkled in the distance. The car slowly rumbled its way to the sanctuary.

The Candy Cane Bakery and Confectionary. A frivolous moniker, but somehow fitting for the town of Green-what-ever-the-second-part-of-the-name-is. Cloaked in darkness, the store sat deserted, but a light shone from a window up above. A spiral staircase led to an apartment over the shop.

Cameron didn't hesitate before turning into the narrow driveway. He had no choice, not unless he preferred to camp in a ditch. He maneuvered the car through a shallow river of mud to what was hopefully a parking space next to an older Toyota. His tires sputtered and protested, seemingly breathing a deep sigh of relief when he turned off the ignition. Of course, he didn't have an umbrella, so on the count of three, he used all his strength to push the door open against the howling wind.

Outside the world thundered like a runaway train, a sea of darkness illuminated by flashes of brilliant electricity. Icy rain pelted his skin, burning his eyes and soaking his clothing. Cameron sprinted through the torrential rain to the staircase, as wind, leaves and branches swirled around him. His $1,500 A. Testoni shoes sank into the mud, and water pelted a Rolex that cost ten times more. He clutched the slippery side rail as he hiked up the stairs two at a time, making it to the front door in thirty seconds flat.

He had no idea of what to expect from the owner of a

store called *The Candy Cane*, as he rang the doorbell. It might take some of his best lawyer skills to convince him – or her – to let him in. That was okay – he was used to convincing people to do what he wanted.

After all, he was always in control.

EAR-SPLITTING RINGING SHOOK THE WORLD, jerking Kaitlyn to consciousness. She shot up, tangled in a sea of blankets, as the terrible intrusion splintered the air once more. Outside, the storm raged, the rain beating a rapid drum, set to the heavy bass of thunder. She scanned the space, yet all was calm and peaceful in the small living room, the air cool, the book still opened to where she'd stopped the night below. As the fogginess lifted, her heart slowed. The "terrible ringing" was nothing more than the doorbell, a jolting yet innocuous interruption to slumber.

Then she froze, relief vanishing like the morning fog. Who would visit at such an hour, through a raging tempest? It could only be one person:

The actor.

She hastily tumbled out of her makeshift bed, nearly falling to the floor in her rush. She still wore her work clothes, but they could no longer claim professional savvy after being slept in on a less-than-spacious sofa. Smoothing herself out as best she could, she strode to the door. How had the actor made it? How had he driven through the horrible weather? How had the plane even landed?

The details didn't matter now. Kaitlyn unlocked the first bolt, but then hesitated. Although his identity was obvious, a single woman living alone must be cautious. "Who's there?"

The man responded just as booming thunder rocked the wooden building to its frame. Beneath the incessant rumbling, she caught only part of a name – Drake, maybe –

and the word "Association." But that was enough. Who else from the Actors Association would call on the eve of a virtual typhoon? She fortified herself, unlocked the door and flung it open.

Whether or not she erred in opening the door, she most certainly miscalculated in opening it wide. A fierce wind instantly grabbed hold of it, slamming the light wood panel against the building with a splintering bang. Kaitlyn grabbed for the knob, yet it slipped in her hand as the tempest bested her in a game of tug-o-war. The rain stung her like a thousand bees, soaking her instantly. Water swept into the apartment, carried on the arms of a strong, unrelenting gale.

The man stood like a ghostly apparition, a shadowy warrior illuminated by electrifying bolts of lightning. Taut limbs froze, and she could do nothing but stare at the two fearsome displays of nature – the raging storm and the man whose power rivalled it. Then with almost superhuman speed, he burst into the apartment, moving into her once private safe haven. He grabbed the door and slammed it shut, as if the wind were no more than a gentle breeze. For the first time, he was clearly visible.

Oh. My. Goodness.

This had to be a mistake. A very big, very muscular, very powerful mistake. This man – no, this giant – could absolutely, positively, 150 billion percent *not* be her new boyfriend. Power radiated from well-built muscles, unrelenting strength focused like a laser beam on her. Oh-please-donotletthisbehim-no.

Domineering and powerful, he towered above her. Not merely tall, he boasted the body of a Medieval warrior, defined by a broad chest, strong arms and a domineering stance. His face held as strong definition as his body, with a chiseled jawline and striking features that brought to life the most handsome male she had ever seen. With deep auburn

17

hair and eyes as green as a cat, he possessed a fierce presence few could match.

This man fit her description perfectly?! Anything but small, he would most certainly never accept the word weak as a description, neither physically nor mentally. And with no time to hire another actor, she had no choice but to pretend to love this man, this warrior who would stay with her in the apartment tonight... alone. Taking a deep breath, she gave the only appropriate response:

"Oh crap."

CHAPTER 2

"Oh crap is absolutely right!" The stranger's eyes blazed golden in emerald depths. "Were you waiting for me to get blown away by the wind or struck by lightning? Perhaps both?" He shook out his jacket, clearly incensed.

He was accusing her of what? Kaitlyn stared. A second later she pulled herself together, channeling shock and fury into pure feminine power. Apparently, this man held not only physical power, but possessed a fiery personality to match. Where was her timid, mild-mannered kitten? Where was the man who would do everything she paid him to do without a problem? This... this Neanderthal was certainly not him.

"Hey, what did you call me?"

Oops, had she said that out loud? Well, too bad. He might be strong and aggressive, but she cowered before no man. Time for her *employee* to learn a few company rules.

"Now wait just a minute!" Crossing her arms over her chest, she glared directly at him. Well, directly at a broad chest straining an expensive suit. She looked up and up and up. That's better – his face. "I'm the one who should be upset!

I gave a very specific description of what I wanted in a man, and you're not even close to what I ordered. And about the door, well I tried to close it, but it wouldn't budge, so it's not my fault you got a little wet. You should be thankful I let you in after waiting all night!" She gave a curt nod and awaited his reply.

Did a shadow of confusion cross the man's face? If so, a cool demeanor quickly replaced it, and even more unexpectedly, relaxed into what could only be described as a warm yet weary smile. The transformation was nothing short of astonishing, turning the cool, unbreakable giant into an almost friendly gentleman. Of course, no man that handsome could ever be trusted.

"You're right." His tone was more amicable, but no less powerful. "I shouldn't be berating you, especially not in your own home. I was merely frustrated by the weather. Now about you expecting me..."

"Yes, I've been waiting for you all night, and don't get me wrong, I'm glad you made it." Kaitlyn softened her voice, even attempted a smile. If he made the effort to play nice, so could she. "It's just I was expecting someone different. I..." Another shrilling noise pierced the air, and she jumped. Her guest was completely unaffected, however, his suave smile in place as he nodded toward the phone. She answered it without taking her eyes off him. "Hello?"

"Ms. Owens, I'm so glad I caught you. This is the receptionist from the Actors Association."

Kaitlyn exhaled pure relief. Perhaps it wasn't too late to get this fixed. Maybe they could switch actors, find someone more suitable. Even though this one started to show a reasonable side, she could never keep him. There was just something about him, something nerve-wracking and powerful and unconquerable. She'd ordered mellow and small, and she meant it. "Thank goodness it's you." Kaitlyn smiled into the phone. "Your actor is here with me right now."

Once more, confusion tinted the man's expression. Taking her lips away from the receiver, she whispered, "It's the Association."

He appeared no less confused, as the receptionist regained Kaitlyn's attention. "He's there with you now?" Surprise, loud and clear, came through the line.

"Yeah, I can't believe he made it in this weather either. But listen…" Kaitlyn lowered her voice, even as the actor loomed too close not to hear. "He's not what I expected. I thought you understood my description. Small, timid, a little geeky."

"You don't think I'm geeky?" an indignant voice spoke. Kaitlyn turned to the actor, who wore an expression of feigned pain. She snorted.

"What I meant…" Kaitlyn couldn't stop the corners of her mouth from lifting upward. "Is I want a nice, mellow guy. This man is not at all what you promised."

"In that case, I'm afraid we can't help you." The receptionist sounded truly regretful – and confused. "He's the closest we have to what you described."

"Are you serious?" Kaitlyn gaped at her guest, somewhat surprised he hadn't yet brandished a sword. He smiled wickedly. "Are you sure you have the right file? It's Kaitlyn Owens. I can pay extra to fly someone else out–"

"No, honey, that's not the problem," the women interrupted gently. "We simply don't have anyone more docile than the actor right in front of you."

Kaitlyn blinked as the *docile* man gazed not-so-innocently around the room, undoubtedly eavesdropping on every word. No one would classify him as small, quiet, mellow or unassuming, and, from the few sentences he uttered, timid and non-aggressive were not within light years of his demeanor. Could he possibly be any different than he seemed, a gentle, agreeable person? Perhaps, but pigs could also be flying outside her window, enjoying the weather. She didn't have time to find out.

"He is really very sweet," the receptionist repeated. "He's..."

"Kaitlyn, can we talk?"

The docile, sweet man loudly interrupted her phone conversation. His next words interrupted her entire existence. "Is there somewhere I can get out of these soaking wet clothes?"

Get out of those soaking wet clothes!?

Yes, please.

In an instant, her mind conjured an image of the powerful man dripping wet, without the little technicality called clothing. He would have smooth, tanned skin, well defined muscles and– "I'm sorry?" she managed a breathless whisper.

His lips quirked up. Had he guessed every wicked thought in her mind? "Is there somewhere I can change out of my wet clothes and into the dry ones I have in my bag?" He pointed towards a small duffel in the corner.

Kaitlyn flushed. Of course, that's what he meant. Of course, she wasn't really, really, really, really disappointed. "The bathroom is that way, and the towels are under the sink." She pointed towards the end of the hall, exhaling in relief when he didn't hesitate before walking away.

She didn't hesitate either. Holding her hand over her mouth, she spoke in a hushed whisper. "I need another man! This actor won't work. Have you seen the size of his…" She breathed out. "Nevermind."

"I'm sorry, I wish I could do more. I–" Click.

Click? Click? Click!?!

"Hello? Hello?" Kaitlyn listened for signs of life, but only a vacuum greeted her. She extended her arm to peer at the handset. The woman hadn't hung up; the signal had died, undoubtedly due to the storm still raging outside. She dropped the phone to the counter. There wasn't time to hire a new actor from another company, and admitting her lies to Cynthia wasn't an option. Her only choice was to proceed with the man currently undressing in her bathroom.

She notched up her chin, fortified herself. She could handle the overconfident, overgrown actor. Steeling her resolve, she plopped down on the couch to await her guest. As soon as the "timid man" returned, she would show him who worked for whom.

CAMERON HAD no trouble finding the single bathroom, which was tinier than the smallest of twelve that graced his mansion. Yet despite its modest dimensions, the room boasted the same charming style as the rest of the home. Good taste had transformed the space into a svelte mixture of elegance and practicality, an admirable and innovative design.

When he first saw the furious woman so flustered, so flushed, so beautiful before him, his well-ordered world had become suddenly unbalanced, a not-so-subtle rearrangement of reality. Perhaps he had been a little harsh about the door... she had, after all, attempted to close it. Usually he acted civilly, but the disaster of an evening had frayed his nerves and piqued his temper. Through it all, one thing loomed as clear as the lightning in the velvet sky:

There was something about this woman.

Something striking, something passionate, something rare, and it hit him like an 18-wheeler. Sure, she was beautiful, even wearing slept-in clothes, but attractive women pursued him all the time, both in a figurative and literal sense. He had long ago grown accustomed to such maneuvering, and even immune. For some reason, this woman was different. Whether by the spark in her deep blue eyes or the way she talked, her fiery personality or her fearless retorts, she captured his attention. Whatever the reason, he needed more information, and as a successful lawyer, he would get it.

After peeling off the soaking clothes and hanging them in the shower to dry, he used a pink towel emblazoned with sparkly cupcakes to dry himself. Actually, the water probably jumped away in fright from the so-sweet-its-scary towel. Thank goodness none of his associates could see him now.

He reviewed the facts as he changed into a tee and Levi's. The woman had hired an actor for some yet-to-be-determined reason, and somehow assumed he was her man. Obviously, he didn't quite match the ordered goods, and this didn't please her at all.

He smiled. No doubt he would be getting a good talking-to when he got back. From the phone conversation, she obviously wanted someone she could control on a six-inch leash, a puppy who would obey her every word. He must have surprised her!

What he should do was clear: Calmly explain the mix-up to his not-so-happy hostess. She would be furious but relieved, and would call the company and request another actor straight away. In all likelihood, she would allow him to spend the night after he told her about his near accident. In the morning, he'd be on his way, never to catch a glimpse of the raven-haired beauty again.

That's what he should do.

For some reason, it wasn't what he was *going* to do.

Never before had he felt such an instant pull to a woman, like a star going red giant. He wanted to learn more about her, her personality, her quirks, her life, but he couldn't do that from a departing vehicle. He only knew her name and that she needed an actor, both gleaned from the phone conversation. He enjoyed mysteries, and even more he liked uncovering them. Plus, she needed an actor, and as a lawyer, he staged shows every day.

For a second, he hesitated, the attorney in him considering all possibilities. What would happen when she found out? Would she go to the police? Could it affect his career, his law firm?

Yet logic reassured him. There was no breaking and entering – she'd invited him in. He hadn't passed himself off as the wrong person; she'd assumed it. He'd make sure she verbally offered him a place to stay.

Even if she discovered the truth, the chances of her actually going to the police were minute. She was doing this for appearance – if she revealed him, she'd expose herself as well. She'd probably just kick him out, and if she didn't, he had pretty impressive free legal counsel. In the worst case, they could work out some sort of settlement – nine times out of ten that kept matters civilized, and he could well afford it.

For the first time in a *very* long time, he would place something above work. It felt strange and disconcerting and yet somehow right. He just finished a big case, so nothing was pressing right now. He'd send a quick email to his colleagues later. They would be curious, but one advantage of being the boss was he didn't have to explain himself.

He was accustomed to operating on his instincts. In this case they told him to explore what could be. He didn't even notice the absence of the ever-present restlessness as he left the bathroom to embark on his new acting career.

THE MAN REENTERED her living room. Thus, Kaitlyn did the only logical action.

She stared.

For about a day and a half.

The first full glimpse of her actor out of soaking wet regalia was like viewing an ice cream sundae with twelve flavors of ice cream, caramel syrup, whipped cream and half the cherries in Florida. Goodness, she sounded like her love-struck friend, but it was his fault for being so savory. He wore a simple black t-shirt stretched across a wide chest, rock hard under the thin, taut cloth, and a pair of well-fitting jeans low on a lean and flat stomach. Corded muscle outlined solid arms and legs, showcasing pure physical power. He seemed even taller than before, more massive, domineering, formidable. Perhaps he was all the cherries in Florida and–

A throat cleared. Powerful arms crossed over a broad chest, and her warrior cast yet another knowing expression.

If she had to accept a gladiator boyfriend, couldn't he at least possess an orangutan-sized brain to balance matters? But no, intelligence glowed in fathomless green-gray eyes, which changed color, mirroring his moods. Now they darkened to almost black. Did he sense the strange emotions he inspired?

Did he feel them, too?

She shouldn't and couldn't go there – he was an employee, nothing more. She wasn't the type to surrender to a man while he asserted control, and obviously this man liked control. It was time to steal it back. "You must feel better now that you're out of your soaking clothes."

"I do feel much better, thank you." He smiled warmly, casting heat through her body.

She blinked, cleared her throat. "Good. To get started, what's your name? You can use your real one or an alias, whatever is more comfortable."

The perfect expression wavered, for just an instant, before his confidence returned. "Drake Alexander at your service, ma'am."

26

"It's a pleasure to meet you, Mr. Alexander." Kaitlyn reached out and shook his hand. He had a sturdy grasp, sparking an almost electric tingling from her fingers to the rest of her body. She withdrew quickly. "I'm Kaitlyn Owens. You know why you're here, I assume."

"Of course," Drake confirmed, "but it's easier to play the part with a fresh reminder of the role."

She bit back a grimace. Why couldn't he simply agree so they could end the disastrous night? "Perhaps tomorrow we can go over–"

"How about tonight? I know it's late, but if I get a head start now, I can absorb the role overnight. It is, of course, your choice."

Assume the role overnight? Like osmosis? Was he serious or trying to be difficult? She sighed, dismissed the latter thought as exhausted paranoia. He wasn't just some stranger who walked in from the street, after all. "Of course. I hired you for a period of one week to pretend to be my loving boyfriend."

Drake's eyes widened, and Kaitlyn stopped. He must have known that part – if not, she was doomed. Yet as quickly as the surprise came, it disappeared. She pressed on, "My cousin is coming to visit, and she expects Mr. Wonderful. She is not a pleasant person, and for reasons I'd rather not discuss, I want her to believe you're this man. Unfortunately, the person I described isn't quite the same as you, as you probably garnered from my earlier phone conversion. Not that there's anything wrong with you," she amended hastily. She wouldn't berate the man simply for being different than expected. "It's just she will be expecting a smallish, timid..."

"Puppy dog?" he supplied.

She squinted her eyes. "No. Just a little, shy..."

"Puppy dog," he said again, this time with a smile.

She growled. Thus far, he was anything but cooperative.

27

Worse yet, she couldn't stop a smile at his playful comment. "May I continue, sir?"

The smile vanished from his lips, but not from his eyes. "My apologies, ma'am. Please go on."

Kaitlyn cleared her throat, "Basically, he's different that you. Now I need you to become this person. You should..."

"Follow your every whim and obey your every word?" He winked.

"Not interrupt every two seconds," she countered.

He grinned widely. And for some strange reason, she did, too. "So…" She straightened. "Are you up for the task?"

The man watched her, boldly taking in everything. How could a mere look affect her so? Her body leapt to awareness, as he finally drawled, "Can you explain the tasks involved in being your loving boyfriend, ma'am?"

Sizzling heat ignited her blood. This was how women fall, and this man probably swatted them down like flies. "There will be no tasks required beyond those specifically laid out to you, sir." She gave a curt nod for emphasis. His eyes glowed with surprise, and to her shock, approval. "Cynthia is expecting a timid, considerate man, and that is precisely what you will portray. Remember, I will be paying you."

For a moment, he said nothing. "And what exactly is the salary, ma'am?"

Newfound suspicion burst forth. Perhaps he required a refresher on the exact role, but to have forgotten his *salary*? Wasn't that what every struggling actor remembered?

Still what ulterior motive could he have? His eyebrows rose when she told him the number, but he said nothing. Would he try to raise his fees, ask for an increment that would put his services out of her price range? If so, he would be disappointed. She'd dipped into her savings as it was; any more would be impossible. Thankfully, he didn't comment on the issue further when he responded, "Can you give speci-fications about the role?"

Of course, he would need more than the command *Be My Boyfriend, Act I.* Yet how to describe the part? "Basically, you need to convince Cynthia you are my boyfriend. You are desperately in love with me, as I am with you. We've been dating for several years. I–"

"Hold on a minute." Drake raised a tanned hand. "Several years is a long time. You realize we would know each other pretty well."

Something unsettled churned in her stomach. "Of course, we'd know each other pretty well. So anyways..." She barreled forward. "I've made arrangements for you to stay at a local hotel. Of course, you can't go tonight, but it should be adequate for tomorrow and the remainder of the–"

"You want me to stay at a hotel?"

Kaitlyn folded her arms. Was he going to fight her on every issue? "Mr. Alexander, you clearly have the wrong idea. I hired you to convince someone you're my boyfriend, not to actually prove the point. There's no need to vie for an Academy Award when not in her company. I am your employer, and you are my employee, and the relationship ends there. No matter what, I require strict professionalism. As much as it might shock you, you are not and will never be invited for anything more. Is that clear?"

His expression changed, but instead of the regretful apology she expected, he smiled like a clever cat who stum-bled upon a bathtub of fish. "Why do you think I'm unhappy with the hotel? Did you assume I was suggesting we explore our roles?"

She stiffened. "I'm not going to explore anything with you."

"Not for a moment did I suspect otherwise."

His smile grew wider, and she faltered. "If that's not why you're so stricken by the prospect of a hotel, then what is it?"

Drake ignored her question. "This cousin of yours, Cynthia, you say she's pretty smart?"

"Enough to make this a challenge," she admitted. "But what does that have to do with your living arrangements?"

"Well, here's the thing." He folded his arms against his chest, tightening the shirt. *Well, look at that–* She swallowed, forced her eyes back to his face, as he continued, "I wasn't concerned about the sleeping arrangements, but instead by the integrity of the role. Isn't Cynthia going to find it strange I live elsewhere when my loving girlfriend lives in this nice apartment with more than enough room for lil ole me?"

"Lil ole you?" She raised an eyebrow.

"All right, big ole me," he revised. "But think about it. We've been dating for *years*, but we don't live together in Greenderland? You see my point, don't you?"

She scowled. "First of all, the city's name is Greenfield, not Greenderland."

Drake merely smiled and shrugged. "My mistake."

"Secondly... secondly..." She breathed out deeply. "You might have a point." But the alternative was entirely unacceptable. "We can't pretend to stay in the same home together!"

"I don't want to pretend. We *should* stay together."

Live with Drake? In the small apartment, with no barrier between him and her? "There's no space," she protested. "There's only one bedroom."

He smiled.

She growled.

He smiled wider.

"Which you will not be sharing with me," she ground out.

Drake laughed. "I figured as much. I'll make do with the couch... at least until she comes."

Kaitlyn decided she disliked the acting profession as a whole.

Still, if she wanted to convince Cynthia she and Drake were Greenfield's own charmed couple, they would have to temporarily share an apartment. Thank goodness he wasn't her "Perfect 10." She could resist six feet plus of pure male. "Fine. But if you try anything," she warned, "you'll be sleeping on the porch if you're lucky and in jail if you're not, Cynthia or no Cynthia. Got it?"

"Got it," Drake agreed. "I'll be the perfect gentleman."

The kitchen clock beeped, startling her. Midnight had long since passed, and her early wakeup was rapidly approaching. Getting to know her employee would have to wait until tomorrow.

"That's enough details for tonight." She rubbed her arms, exhaustion weakening strained muscles. "If I don't go to bed soon, I'll sleep through Cynthia's entire visit. Which actually isn't a horrible idea."

"I'd much rather be awake." He grinned roguishly. "I'm intrigued to see what happens."

Did actors always enjoy their roles so much? Ignoring slight suspicion and not-so-slight unease, she retrieved a pillow and blanket for her guest. He grasped the soft quilted fabric, just over her hands. And for just a moment… he didn't let go.

His eyes were like the sea, fathomless and endless, and impossible to escape once they captured you in their powerful depths. Her breath hitched as a million unnamed questions surged, with one at its crescendo: What was he doing to her?

"I suppose it's goodnight, then." She pulled her hands back, unsuccessfully for a moment, until he finally released her. She didn't wait for a reply before she turned and walked – okay, fled – to the safety of her bedroom. She firmly shut the door, then stood pressed against it for seconds and then minutes, before she finally changed into a nightgown and slipped into bed.

Despite her exhaustion, sleep proved elusive. Minutes and then hours passed, and she remained awake, as the man who slept yards away consumed every thought. Had she met him on the street, actor-for-hire would have been the last profession she'd imagine for him. Perhaps CEO, lawyer, *dictator*, something in which his aggressive nature and powerful demeanor would fit right in. What made him choose such an ill-suited career path?

Worse yet, he'd lodged himself in her psyche, despite their recent acquaintance. When she finally fell into a restless sleep, she dreamed of him, lucid images that remained as she repeatedly awoke during the stormy night. Each time, she tried in vain to picture a small, submissive man nothing like the powerful Drake Alexander. And each time she failed, with no power over her mind's conjuring.

Nor over the small smile that escaped as she once again dreamed of Drake.

CHAPTER 3

*T*hursday morning arrived heralded by aqua skies and a bright, shining sun. Outside the window, the lush, green farmland stretched, a dew-covered world blooming with the rebirth that only comes following a particularly turbulent storm. The air smelled sweet and fragrant, a heady mixture of gardenias and the honeyed delight of baked goods.

Despite the land's renewal, Kaitlyn awoke anything but refreshed. Jerked into consciousness by a blasting used car commercial on her radio alarm, she rested quietly in bed, trapped in a state of exhaustion. She closed her eyes, clinging to the small amount of peace that came in the early morning, before the hectic pace of the day began.

"Rise and shine! It's the early bird that fools the cousin!"

Kaitlyn gasped, scrambling up at the booming voice. Drake stood in the doorway, tall, handsome and all sorts of confident, like he'd stepped from one of Allison's gossip websites. He was already crisply dressed, his dark hair falling in soft waves and emerald eyes sparkling with intelligence and humor.

"What are you doing?" She gasped. "Do you have any idea what time it is?"

"Time to get moving," Drake pointed toward the alarm. "I figured you didn't want to waste any time lying around. I heard your alarm, so I knew were up."

"That didn't mean I wanted to get out of bed. How could you just barge into my room? It's...it's inappropriate!" She folded her arms across her chest. The move lifted her thin nightgown, outlining *everything*. With a hiss, she dove under the covers. "Drake Alexander, leave this room right now!"

She growled as the actor chuckled. "Of course," he said solemnly. But laughter edged his tone as he sauntered out of the room and shut the door.

That impossible man! Drake was playing his part a little too soon and a lot too well. It had better be his way of preparing for the role.

She had a sinking feeling otherwise.

KAITLYN WAS NOT a happy candy maker. As she entered the living room dressed in a severe black business suit that would have sobered a mortician, she fashioned a stern look and a crisp gait. Only Drake remained unaffected, as he gave her a thorough perusal, from the tips of her toes to the top of her head and *everything* in between. Her skin pinkened under his scrutiny, his gaze brushing shivers on her skin. She cleared her throat, fortified herself. He had no right to unbalance her. Boldly, she returned the gaze.

Her mouth dried.

Her would-be suitor wore a sharp *Armani* suit, crisp and dark and fit to perfection. Although it covered him completely, it did nothing to hide his size or strength. He seemed even more impressive wearing the expensive outfit, tall and broad, proud and fierce, his towering strength almost tangible.

She exhaled slowly. He was only a man – a mouth-watering, caramel covered, candy apple of a man.... Stop! She forced a severe gaze. "Mr. Alexander, about this morning..."

"Drake," The man interloped with a pointed look. "Would you talk to your One and Only like you talk to your accountant?"

He had a point. The ruse would be up the first time she called him Mr. Alexander in front of Cynthia. She needed to grow accustomed to his first name. "Drake, about this morning–"

"Yes, about this morning," he once again interrupted, "I want to apologize for my rash and inappropriate behavior. A gentleman should never enter a lady's bedroom uninvited, especially when she might be wearing... bedroom attire." She parted her lips, as he continued, "You have obviously been frustrated by my actions, and for that I am truly sorry." He stopped, and then seemingly as an afterthought added, "I also apologize for interrupting you a second time. You were saying..." He looked at her expectantly.

Kaitlyn's cheeks burned. The infernal man had done it again! Every time she planned to stand up in the name of decent women everywhere, he made it impossible. What could she say without sounding petulant? "Thank you. I think you covered everything," she said primly.

A ghost of a smile played on his lips, but it vanished quickly. There was no time to dwell. In thirty-six hours, they would have to absorb a lifetime of knowledge about each other, details that normally took years to learn. She would have to convince Cynthia he had invaded her heart and dreams. After last night, the final task might not be too difficult – the rest, she wasn't so sure. Yet the sooner they got started, the more they could accomplish. "We have a long day ahead of us."

"True." He flexed his arms. "But first, how about a nice breakfast?"

She dragged her gaze away from corded arms. "You want me to cook?" If he expected her to be his personal chef just because she owned a bakery, he would be disappointed. She was far too busy to craft an extensive meal, and with her cousin's imminent arrival, she'd be lucky to have time to eat.

Her cooking was not, however, what he had in mind. "Not at all. I like to cook. I used to do it all the time when I was a kid." His smile was genuine, wistful and almost boyish, as if he was remembering a sweetly nostalgic time. For some reason, it seemed like he didn't wear the expression often.

"That was a long time ago." He shook his head. "Since I've become an adult, I haven't had time to cook. I pay someone to prepare my meals."

She lifted an eyebrow. "Pay someone? Actors must do a lot better than candy shop owners."

His smile vanished. When it reappeared seconds later, it seemed less sincere, more practiced. "I'm joking, of course. Actually, I can't afford streaming on what I earn, let alone a chef. I was referring to prepared meals, you know, frozen dinners."

Kaitlyn nodded, although the explanation seemed somehow insufficient. "Are you sure you want to do this?" Now if he told her he wanted wrestle a bear while watching football and driving a racecar, she would believe it. "You just don't seem like a guy who would enjoy cooking, but you might very well be." She cocked her head playfully to the side. "Who knows? You might even surprise me."

"It's my specialty," he returned with a mischievous grin she couldn't help but return. This man was going to be trouble, in all sorts of ways.

"Cooking?" she teased.

"No. Surprises." He winked. "But don't worry. I'm pretty good at whipping something out of nothing. It'll probably take me an hour to create my masterpiece, so feel free to go about your morning."

Leaving was a good idea. She needed to get away from this kitchen and this man, with his quick wit, roguish grin and all-too-charming smile. Her employees were tending to the store today, but it couldn't hurt to check in and make sure everything was proceeding smoothly. And if she moved just a little quicker than normal, no one was there to notice.

KAITLYN WAS DELIGHTFUL.

There was no better word to describe the vivacious woman, although there were many other words he could use: lovely, smart, spirited. Despite their short acquaintance, something had flared between them, something that demanded attention. She clearly sensed it too, although by how she repeatedly fled, it was obvious she didn't want to feel it. Yet, it lurked between them, and would not be denied.

It deserved exploration.

He never imagined he'd skip work to be in a small-town apartment, cooking breakfast while pretending to be someone's fake boyfriend. And if somehow he convinced himself of that possibility, he never thought he'd enjoy it this much. His work as an environmental lawyer was vital and meaningful, yet it was nice to create something so simple and yet so vital as sustenance. The urge to treat and surprise her rose, as the scent of sizzling potatoes filled the small kitchen. Yet it wasn't nearly as strong as the desire to learn more about her. Fortunately, he had a whole week…

Or perhaps far longer.

· · ·

DRAKE LOOKED HAPPY, content and strangely at home. As Kaitlyn strolled back into her apartment, her gaze snagged the confident man who roamed her kitchen like he belonged there. Then she stopped, staring at the sumptuous array of food spread on her small table. How had he done so much in so little time?

A few eggs and meager groceries had transformed into a full country breakfast, including fluffy yellow omelets with all the trimmings, golden brown toast with sweet cream butter and a juicy fresh fruit assortment. Steak cut potatoes sizzled on the stove, casting a mouth-watering scent, while thick slices of French toast cooked on the griddle.

It was a veritable feast, yet the most delicious fare had nothing to do with the food, but with the tantalizing man cooking it. He'd removed his jacket and rolled up his sleeves, revealing muscular forearms and tanned skin. The shirt stretched taut against his broad chest, and the pants molded to his sturdy legs, as he moved with confidence and ease, master of his domain. A lock of hair fell across his forehead, above chiseled features. He was strength defined, handsome and so very striking.

She closed her eyes, opened them with newfound resolve. She couldn't afford wandering thoughts. He was only here temporarily, and once Cynthia left, so would he. She forced herself into the room and retrieved two floral plates from the cupboard. "This looks great."

"Thank you." Drake turned off the heat and lifted the pan from the range. He brought it over and served the eggs with a bright orange spatula. "I figured we could use a little energy today. I know I'm not what you expected."

She chuckled, yet for just a moment, she was glad he was here. "Let's eat, and we'll commence our learn-as-much-as-you-can-in-36-hours marathon."

He gave them each a healthy portion of the food, then

held out her chair. Who said chivalry was dead? Ah yes, it had been her. Yet he was the perfect gentleman, and even waited for her to taste the food before he began. As expected, the scrumptious food practically melted in her mouth. The eggs were light and fluffy, the potatoes crisp and the fruit perfectly ripe. They ate in comfortable silence, and minutes passed before the taciturn camaraderie broke.

"This is delicious." She savored another tasty morsel, then another. Finally, she placed down her fork. "I couldn't have another bite."

"Thank you." He sipped his orange juice and lowered his own utensils. "Hopefully, Cynthia will be similarly impressed."

"Hopefully, Cynthia will be long gone before she has the chance to enjoy breakfast." She raised her glass.

"Hear, hear." An ever-so-sly smile eased his strong features. "So boss, ready to begin?"

She couldn't help but smile at his boyish expression. What an enigma he was, so serious and strong one moment, so playful the next. Who was the real Drake Alexander? Soon, she would find out.

She rubbed her hands together. "Here's how we'll do this. Basically, you need to learn all about me and we both need to learn about the fictional character you'll be playing. I'll start with some simple facts. First..."

"I object."

She froze in mid-sentence. "You can't object."

"I just did."

She narrowed her eyes, reminded herself that throwing French toast at actors was poor form. "What could you possibly object to?"

"The plan. It's unsatisfactory." He crossed his arms over his chest, a motion that gave the impression of a brick wall. A very attractive, unmovable brick wall.

If this was the meekest man at the entire *Actors Association*, what were the strong ones like? "Since you find my methods so objectionable, could you please explain exactly what bothers you. You do know why you were hired, don't you?"

"Oh, absolutely." He nodded succinctly. "It's not the entire plan I object to."

She should probably consider herself fortunate. He showed no unease as he continued, "Obviously, I need to learn all about you to convince your cousin of our deep love for each other. I simply object to the creation of a fictional character for me."

She lifted her arms. "But we have to make up a character for you. We can't go with traveling actor who lives out of town and knows nothing about me. No offense, but you're the exact antithesis of what I described."

Drake rolled his eyes. "I remember – Marshmellowman with an emphasis on the mellow."

Kaitlyn grimaced, and he laughed. "Of course, we need to come up with a fictitious set of credentials for me – occupation, activities I partake in, things like that. But as far as my personal character goes, that's staying the same. This is who I am, and this is who I'm staying."

"But that's impossible," she growled. "I told Cynthia that..."

"I know what you told her," he interrupted, "and I'm truly sorry. I just can't pretend to be something I'm not. I'm an..."

"Wait let me guess. You're an arteeest."

A smile rounded his lips. "Exactly. So it's your call. Either I act like me, or you hire some poodle to play the role. Literally."

Why that domineering, arrogant, too-handsome for his own good... ahem. She didn't have time to hire another actor, or even a poodle for that matter, and he knew it. With no other option, she would have to give in.

40

But only on this point. He mustn't think he would always get the best of her. One usually got further with charm and cunning than with argument. Time to beat Mr. Drake Alexander at his own game.

"Why are you smiling?"

"Oh, nothing," she hedged. "It's just I forgot to mention your profession. You see, Cynthia seems to have gotten the idea you are...well she believes..." She paused for dramatic measure. "You're my personal assistant."

Silence.

Then..."Personal assistant?" Drake echoed. "I'm the personal assistant of the owner of *The Candy Cane?*"

"And a very good one at that." Kaitlyn winked. "I told her you're exceptional at sorting measuring spoons."

Danger swirled. Time to finish her sweet revenge before the volcano erupted. "As a compromise, you can keep your personality. So long as it goes along with your position."

Drake folded his arms across his chest, stretching the thin shirt against formidable muscles. He studied her slyly, and she suppressed a shiver. Was he baking a plan of his own? "No problem," he replied smoothly.

Her confidence wavered at his I'm-back-in-control-and-there's-nothing-you-can-do-about-it expression. There was no backing away now. "Now that that is settled, I'll start by telling you about myself."

Only she hesitated once more. Despite the necessity of sharing personal information, it seemed strange telling her life story to a stranger, especially a man like Drake Alexander. She hadn't a choice, however. She couldn't fabricate a life story Cynthia already knew in full detail.

"My name is Kaitlyn Leeann Owens," she started. "I'm 28 years old, birthday October 31st – not a word please." The sides of his mouth quirked up, but he wisely stayed quiet. "I have a degree in Business Administration, which I used to open this store six years ago."

"That's impressive," Drake commented. "You were pretty young to pursue a business venture, but it's obviously paying off now. By the size of the crowd downstairs and the professionalism of the entire set-up, I'd say you're doing pretty well."

Kaitlyn couldn't stop a flush. "I do all right."

"You're doing better than all right." He pointed through the window to where customers had pooled outside the shop. "Have you thought about opening another?"

Kaitlyn hesitated. They'd wandered off topic, yet she found herself sharing more. "It has been on my mind," she admitted. "The store has been profitable for a long time, and soon it'll reach its potential. I believe another store could be just as lucrative, plus an old-fashioned confectionary is a wonderful asset to a town. I would love to bring that to more people. But that's sort of the problem. Greenfield is too small for another candy store – I would have to open it somewhere else."

"Is that a challenge?" queried Drake. "I passed a lot of small towns on my way here, one right after the other."

"That's true." She nodded. "Several close towns are suitable, but I'm worried about what would happen if I opened another. Would I neglect this shop? Would I become overwhelmed by trying to do both? Of course, the money would be nice, but it's not really a necessity in my life. I'm not sure I want to take that chance."

"I understand your concerns." His voice was warm and genuine. "Opening the store must have been a challenge, and now that it's a success, you don't want to jeopardize that. But think of all the rewards."

"Of course," she conceded. "But I'm worried it might be a little too much for me to handle myself."

"That's why you have employees, and besides, you don't seem like the type of woman who would let 'too much' or 'too risky' stop her from anything." He gave her a gentle nudge. "Right boss?"

Kaitlyn chuckled. It was true – she didn't let challenges rein her in. "I'm not the type to be stopped," she agreed softly. "Thanks for the advice." An actor seemed an unlikely candidate for a business advisor, but his commonsense responses gave her much to ponder. She rubbed her hands. "We'd better get back to the learning session."

"You're in charge."

Even as she smiled again, it didn't quite ring true. Clearly, this wasn't a man who surrendered control, which again raised the question of why he was in this position. It was something to consider later. "I grew up in Greenfield with my parents and two brothers, although they now live a couple of hours away. I always wanted to run my own business. My favorite movie is..."

KAITLYN SPOKE about her life in animated detail, capturing Cameron despite every attempt to remain unaffected. The vibrant woman was alluring in a thousand ways, authentic, down-to-earth, and yet somehow infinitely fascinating. He'd never met such a captivating woman, even among the successful entrepreneurs, actresses and socialites, rich and powerful ladies who commanded power and position.

None could compare to the beautiful candy maker.

He smiled inwardly, remembering her announcement of his role as "personal assistant." She'd been lying. After years as a successful lawyer, he had developed an excellent sense for the truth, and he'd bet the firm she hadn't told Cynthia any such thing. His "job" was simply payback for being difficult.

He didn't mind being her assistant. An assistant knew his employer – what she did, and even more, who she did it with. It would give him the chance to discover all about the woman with the mysterious effect on him. He couldn't have concocted a better plan himself.

He still didn't understand his own behavior when it came to her, starting with this morning. He had barged into a woman's room without an invitation. Actually, it was more than without an invitation – he clearly wasn't welcome in the sleeping woman's private sanctuary. But when he heard the alarm, he hadn't been able to stop himself. And then once he got there, it just seemed natural to joke with the sleepy temptress.

What he hadn't expected was the spell she immediately cast on him. Of course, the sight of the beautiful brunette would have made the strongest of men weak with desire, yet far more than creamy skin and delectable curves attracted him. She was charming and clever, lively and delightful, and she made him want to learn everything about her. And this was after knowing her for a single night.

He'd had a close call when he accidentally mentioned his personal chef. Thank goodness he hadn't brought up the gardener! Of course, a traveling actor wouldn't employ a household staff. Good fortune had prevented Kaitlyn from reading too much into his slip. She had accepted his excuse, but hesitantly, and more mistakes would not go unnoticed.

She affected him in ways he dared not explore. Their short conversation made him practically nostalgic, the discussions about cooking whispers from the past. He didn't think about his childhood often – it represented an entirely different lifetime from his fast-paced life. Yet the pensive insight was not entirely unpleasant. And it occurred by grace of his new employer.

His employer was as sharp as the top minds he sparred

against, and just as savvy. He would have to watch himself around the woman who was proving to be far more than a beautiful smile. She was intelligent, wickedly so. And the one thing sexier than a great body was a great mind. Kaitlyn possessed both.

She thought he was there to pretend to be her boyfriend. Instead, he was there to discover why she affected him.

Then he might just pursue something *more*.

CHAPTER 4

"*A*re you listening?" Kaitlyn touched Drake lightly on the shoulder.

His head snapped up. "Of course."

"So by the time I got to high school, I–" A shrill ringing interrupted her, and she started. She relaxed a moment later. "That's the doorbell. Excuse me for a moment."

Who was calling at such an early hour? Perhaps it was one of her workers, even though they typically used the inside entrance. Only when she peered through the peephole, a small, thin man with a balding head stared back through the tiny portal. She opened the door and smiled. "Can I help you?"

"I'm terribly sorry for bothering you, miss." The man had a nasal voice and an uncertain tone, as if he were embarrassed by the simple art of talking. He stood only an inch or two taller than her petite frame, friendly enough, and more than safe. "I know it's early, and I'm not even sure I have the right place."

Kaitlyn softened. "Who are you looking for? Maybe I can lead you to your destination."

"Well, I think I'm supposed to help you."

A sudden movement caught Kaitlyn's attention. A very determined Drake hovered at the room's edge, his eyes blazing. Then he was coming towards her, faster and faster. "Drake, what are you–"

Before she could finish the question, he replied.

It was not a verbal response.

Drake captured her lips – and her. She froze for a second's sliver before surrendering to the passion-filled haze, captive to his sensual administrations. He caressed her, soft and gentle, tenderly coaxing her to respond. She could do nothing but answer his call, matching his motions, parrying a sensual duel.

The kiss deepened, as passion replaced sweetness, sensuality joined tenderness. Excitement and heat sizzled as electricity passed between them, chemistry pure and simple, undeniable and unbreakable. He had initiated the kiss, but she now returned it, bolding probing his mouth. They became closer yet as he wrapped his arms around her, pulling her softness into the solid rock of his chest, in power and *possession*.

Somewhere deep within her, a small part of her mind still functioned. This man had somehow enraptured her. Any other woman would fall, but she would not. She would demand answers, order an explanation.

As soon as she was done with the kiss.

No. She must regain her senses and her control. Yet wondrous sensations bombarded her, commanding her to continue, to savor this man. She tapped into the last of her control, and with all her strength, drew back. Immediately a void assailed her, a coldness like midnight winter in the Arctic wilderness. She touched sensitive fingers to swollen lips as her conqueror drew back. Although he initiated the kiss, he appeared as surprised as she felt.

For a moment, they just stared at each other, silent save for shallow breathing and rapidly beating hearts. The doorway was empty, her diminutive visitor no longer in sight. Not that she blamed him for leaving, mustering only passing curiosity regarding his identity and purpose. She wouldn't chase him down, not when she had a much more commanding issue with which to deal.

Her voice breathless, she spoke first, "What in the world was that?"

Drake stood still, his expression stoic and pensive. A second later a mischievous gleam lit. "Wasn't that your cousin?"

She stared. "Did that look like a Cynthia?"

He tapped his chin, nodded. "Come to think of it, he did look a little like a Cynthia."

Seriously? She should demand an immediate explanation, challenge why he did it and how he affected her. But unfortunately, most of all, she wanted another kiss. Another and another and another.

She shook her head, clearing thoughts clouded by passion. This was the trouble she got for letting a man like Drake into her home. "I assure you, that was not Cynthia."

"Are you certain?"

"Yes."

"Like one hundred percent sure?"

"Um... yeah."

"How?"

"Because Cynthia is a woman."

Drake shrugged. "Good point."

Good point? Good point!?

This was going to be a very long week.

. . .

"CAN YOU REMEMBER ALL THAT?" Kaitlyn asked a few hours later, her voice tinged with doubt. She'd thrown half a lifetime's worth of information at her unlikely savior, more than anyone could learn in a month, much less a day. Hopefully he would recall enough to convincingly play the role.

"I think I've got it," Drake replied with his typical confidence. "You've lived a full life."

Yes, she had. Yet for the first time, something seemed missing. "I don't have everything." She clamped her lips shut. Where had that come from? "My life is great." She tore her gaze away. "Perfect."

He needed to pull back, and now. If he continued to hover, she might just admit something to him, and herself. After a brief hesitation, he relaxed, but the challenge never left. He was clearly not yet finished, not with the subject.

Not with her.

She steered the conversation back to business. "Are you ready to create the new and improved Drake Alexander?"

"New and improved?" He grimaced, and she exhaled. For now, serious conversation was over. "Tell me the truth." He held up his hands. "Do you really think I need improving?"

In spite of everything, she laughed. "Yes!"

He pressed a hand to his heart, the epitome of wounded pride. "How will I ever get over your cruelty?"

She laughed again. "Through unemployment, unless you're a better actor than this little performance demonstrates."

"Now even my position is in danger?" he asked in horrified tones. "Then it's time to get back to business. Now let me tell you about Drake Alexander. He is a very serious man. He is also very successful and leads hundreds of people–"

"Now hold on just a moment." He was trying to take control, and with a ridiculous story Cynthia would never believe. "I'll create my boyfriend's biography."

49

He narrowed his eyes. "I thought we agreed I would display my own charming personality."

"We agreed you could be yourself," she confirmed, "but I get to decide your interests and activities."

He crossed his arms, tightening his muscles. It stole her attention more than she'd ever admit, even as he continued, "I have no desire to be head polka instructor at the Y."

"I'm not going to make you head polka instructor." She paused. "Just an assistant."

A deep baritone laugh rumbled from his chest, and her lips twitched into a smile. He stepped closer, and the laughter died. "I spend my entire life predicting what people will do, and I'm usually very good at it. But with you..." His voice trailed off, and he withdrew his hand. "Let's just say you surprise me."

She drew in a shaky breath. "How about a deal? I'll let you dictate your hobbies right down to whether you're a polka instructor if–" She gave him her best business look. "You're cooperative when Cynthia is around."

He grimaced. "I'd prefer to be assistant polka instructor."

"Come on," she prodded. "I'm not asking you to adhere to my every whim. You just need to be a little more agreeable. You should find that easy in your line of work."

He was silent for a moment. "All right," he agreed. "I will do my best to not be overbearing and instead–" His lips curled in distaste. "Compromise."

She laughed. Clearly, the man was accustomed to getting what he wanted. It seemed a strange expectation for an actor-for-hire. "Ok then, tell me about Drake Alexander."

She listened as he outlined his interests and activities. They actually sounded fascinating, however they fit his profession like a dinosaur in a tea shop. Why had a man like him – powerful, dominant, authoritative – become an actor-for hire? The mystery deepened with every word.

When he finally finished, she got up and stretched. "I think that's enough for now. Why don't we take a break?"

He shook his head. Why had she thought he would agree? "We should consider other aspects of the relationship. If you want to convince her, we can't just know each other's hobbies. We need to act like we're together."

"What do you mean–" She froze as images flashed, memories of their recent kiss. "That's fine." Why had her voice ascended in pitch? "No problem, of course." Even higher. "It's great." Fantastic. Now she sounded like a chipmunk.

"Don't you think we should practice those assumed things?"

Practice?

Practice!?

His words electrified her, searing her blood and firing her senses. Was he trying to elicit a reaction or being serious? He couldn't expect her to kiss on demand. And why did the idea sound so appealing? "You've got to be kidding."

He stepped closer. "We should practice being close to each other."

"Being close to each other," she echoed. That didn't sound too bad.

"Hugging."

Relief flooded her. "No problem."

"Kissing."

Relief crashed, burned and died a fiery death. Hugging was one thing, but kissing? She barely broke away the first time. Was he trying to unbalance her? Assert his control? Did he want another kiss as much as she did?

Regardless of motives, she would have to be close to him, hug him and even kiss him, in order to convince Cynthia. How could they claim to be in love and not show it? Of course, they could improvise, but she had to garner more control than she displayed earlier. Right now, she would accost him if he so much as gave her a friendly peck on the cheek. She needed to be comfortable showing affection without grabbing her club and dragging him to the nearest cave.

Practice was definitely called for, if only to see how they would respond to each other. "You're right," she agreed on a deep breath. "We need to practice." She edged nearer to him, fighting dual urges to approach and flee. Admiration tinted his expression, and he held out his hand. She touched his palm, and he enveloped her fingers. His hand was warm and firm, and his commanding presence surrounded her in possessive strength.

"This seems pretty natural." She wiggled her hand slightly, but he did not let go. For a moment, she stood still, strangely comfortable, with no desire to break the contact.

"Ready to try hugging?"

Inwardly she smiled. After the kiss they shared earlier, hugging seemed as safe as a swim in the kiddie pool. "All right." She faced him, so close she could see the soft rise and fall of his chest. Drake's breath fanned her hair as he reached out and captured her, closer and closer until he completely enveloped her in his grasp. At first, she stiffened, but then she relaxed, returning the hug, pushing into the solid wall of muscle. Like two pieces of a jigsaw puzzle, they fit together perfectly.

"This isn't so tough," she whispered. "Convincing Cynthia we feel something won't be difficult at all."

"Not at all," he murmured.

It should definitely fool Cynthia, because it was fooling her. Finally, she broke the embrace, stepped back as a sense of loss enveloped her. "That was adequate."

"Perfectly fine." Drake's voice held little emotion, but

something potent simmered just below the surface. "Want to try the next part again? You know the…"

"Kissing." She licked dry lips. "I suppose we have no choice. Just like the actors do in the movies. Piece of cake." Piece of cake? Tasting him would be easy; stopping before she devoured the whole delicacy would be difficult.

"Just like in the movies." Drake reached towards her. She didn't move as her breathing came in soft, rapid pants, and her heart beat like a runaway train. He grazed her cheek with the pad of his finger as he captured her in his gaze. Her eyes fluttered closed as he descended and then…

Fireworks.

A slow and gentle caress, a delicious kiss. She wrapped her arms around him, surrendering to the sensations he wrought. His lips were firm and pliant, his hands masterful, as he caressed sensitive spots. She was drowning, but it didn't matter. The touches were too wonderful, the feelings endlessly exquisite. A connection formed as moments and minutes passed, the outside world melting away. Whatever resolve she possessed disappeared; in its place remained pure instinct.

A sharp ringing pierced the air. She ignored it at first, but it continued again and again, oblivious to the chaos. And, suddenly, the spell broke.

She reeled, not in reaction to the ringing phone, but at the sudden realization of what a simple kiss had done. It consumed her, vanquishing the world beyond. It took all her strength to pull back, and then it was over, but in a way it never would be. Somehow everything was different.

Neither said a word. Neither moved, not even when the answering machine clicked on, or when a voice started to speak. She inhaled shakily, fought for words.

"I… I think we have that down." Her voice was breathless, her tone light. If only she could hide his effect on her, but it was as obvious as the flush undoubtedly heating her cheeks. The clever man gazed at her, as if he understood her every thought. She couldn't hide from him.

She may not be able to undo the past, but she could fix the present and shape the future. This mustn't go any further. She didn't have time for a man, especially not an overbearing, authoritative would-be boyfriend who stole all control. Thus, despite her traitorous mind clamoring for one – or a thousand – more practice sessions, she shrugged. "I don't think we need another rehearsal."

He narrowed his eyes almost imperceptibly. Did he guess her thoughts didn't quite match her words? Would he ask for more? Her heart quickened, even as he nodded. "I think we've got it. For now."

She bit back a shudder. Enough for *now*. Which meant there would be more later. How much more? What type of more? Could more involve whipped cream?

"Good!" She needed to get away from him and the ridiculous urges he inspired. "Since we're done with er… practice, I have some errands to run. I should be back by dinnertime. We can go over the information then." She was rambling, but it didn't matter. She grabbed her purse, retrieved her keys and headed for the door.

"Hold on a moment," a powerful voice called from behind. "You're leaving? I thought you cleared your schedule to prepare for your cousin."

She had, but she needed a little time away. Like a year or a thousand. She made it to the door, forced herself to turn. "I remembered some things I need to do–" *Like write I will not imagine Drake covered in whipped cream a hundred times.* "But I think we covered everything." Only, actually, she wished she covered more. Of him, that was. In whipped cream. She pressed forward, "You're welcome to stay or go out, whatever you'd like."

"Actually, I was hoping you would accompany me on an errand," he replied evenly.

"I wish I could." She unlocked the door. "I'm sure you'll get along fine without me!"

"I guess I'll just have to choose my wardrobe without you."

Kaitlyn was five steps out the door when his words resonated through the hallway. She froze, traced her steps back. "I'm sorry?"

He moved closer. "My wardrobe."

"What about it?" Thus far his clothing had been acceptable, or even above what she'd expected. It was the one thing that had gone right. "I assume you brought appropriate attire."

"Actually, I didn't bring any attire," he replied calmly. "What you saw yesterday and today, that's it."

Stay calm. One... two...three... Nope. "How could you come to a multi-day acting position with only one change of clothes? Cynthia is bound to start noticing very, very quickly."

"I didn't plan it this way." He shrugged. "Let's just say the thunderstorm complicated matters. Don't worry, I can grab some clothing from the local store. I'll see you tonight."

Don't worry? The acting company specified all character-related expenses would be hers, and this certainly qualified. Calculating her income for the month, she cringed. They would definitely have to be tight on what they bought. Which meant she was going on a little shopping spree.

"You don't have to wait for me." The actor donned his coat. "I can lock the door from the inside."

She gritted her teeth. "I'm coming with you. And–" she cut off his impending response, "I don't want to hear a word. Got it?"

Drake smiled, but said nothing.

.   .   .

KAITLYN HAD NEVER RIDDEN in a Porsche before, but even she could appreciate the marriage of comfort and racecar-like agility. The inside was sleek and smooth, with gleaming controls and plush butter seats, the perfect foil to the scenery racing outside the tinted windows. Suspicion soon tempered the pleasure, however, as pedestrians stopped to stare at the car, and other drivers gave them second and third looks. How could an actor-for-hire afford a luxury vehicle? She couldn't ask... or could she? "This is a classy car," she said lightly. "Most of your clients must be wealthier than me."

He gave a short nod, yet said nothing, as the seconds stretched. Clearly, he had no plans to elaborate. Time to try again. "I don't know a great deal about sports cars," she remarked. "What year is this?"

This time he did speak, but only to directly answer her question. "It's this year. Brand new."

Her curiosity soared, but she couldn't find out more without blatantly asking personal questions. Only she didn't have to. "The company arranged for me to have it," he offered with a wry glance. "It's not mine."

Of course – the company. It didn't make sense for it to be his, and it wasn't. Strange they would give him such an expensive car, but then again they were a full service firm. Of course, he was only here for a week.

And suddenly a week seemed like a very short time indeed.

She almost missed the turn-off for the store. At the last minute, she pointed towards a small one-story building off the side of the road, and Drake snapped to turn the wheel. He gave the shop a dubious glance as he pulled into a gravel parking lot and glided to a halt. "This is the source of my new wardrobe?"

Kaitlyn wasn't surprised by his attitude. Newcomers to town were often fooled by the simple veneer of the "Greenfield Clothing Store." No larger than her apartment, the quaint white villa featured soft wood paneling, green shutters and a long wraparound porch. A small sign gave the only indication it was more than a family home, which it had been for over a century beforehand. Now it housed rows upon rows of clothing, packed impossibly yet impeccably in the meager space, run by the best seamstress in three counties. At least that's what Kaitlyn and the residents of Greenfield knew. From the skeptical look of her shopping companion, he clearly didn't feel the same way.

He would discover that soon enough, likely within thirty seconds of meeting the eccentric Miss Ida Lane, but now an opportunity beckoned. And as a successful entrepreneur, she couldn't let an opportunity slip by. "You don't think you're going to find anything?"

Drake remained silent as he exited the car and opened her door, but his thoughts were obvious. "It isn't quite what I expected, but that's all right." His tone was cordial as he stepped toward the store. "I'll make do."

"It doesn't meet your standards?" she persisted, making no move to follow her partner's footsteps.

He turned around, chuckling lightly. "It's all or nothing, is it?" A genuine smile softened his strong features. "Okay, then." He looked again towards the small villa. "No, I honestly don't think I'm going to find anything. I was thinking more of a mall or department store. The Greenfield Clothing Store is probably not going to have my style."

Kaitlyn didn't mention that Miss Ida developed styles *before* they emerged in the exclusive catalogs. Instead, she prepared for checkmate. "Would you care to make a friendly wager on that?" she asked innocently.

Drake's eyes narrowed ever so slightly. His instincts were too good. Now she stood as tall as she could. "Unless you're worried you're going to lose."

He straightened, a predatory gleam darkening his expression. "I never lose." It was a simple statement of fact, an assertion, which always came true. Or so he thought. "What are the terms?"

The terms. Here it was – a veritable gold mine. A bet she could not lose, now what to ask for? An uninvited image raced through her mind, of exactly what she would like to do with this man, and what she would like this man to do to *her*. Pushing that image away, she offered the next best thing, "If you find an entire closetful of clothes, then I win. If you don't find anything or even if you select just a few things, you win. And the winner.... the winner..."

"The winner gets to make plans for tonight."

Make plans for the night? It wasn't a bad idea. There were some things he wouldn't go along with unless he had to. "All right," she agreed. "That's an acceptable wager, however we need rules."

"Like I can't decide our plans will consist of me taking you back to your place and..."

"Don't you dare." *Even if it was exactly what she wanted.* She cleared her throat. "It has to be completely G-rated."

"G-rated? Not even PG?" Bemusement betrayed his disappointment. "All right," he agreed, "G-rated it is. But all I was going to say was..."

"I don't want to hear it." She pivoted towards the shop, putting him to her back so he couldn't see the smile. And she was most definitely happy he couldn't see her heated expression when he said, "I merely wanted more practice."

CHAPTER 5

*A*s Drake stepped through the doorway, his expression remained neutral, with no hint of what transpired behind those deep emerald eyes. Yet surely he sensed his wager was a poor one, as he viewed the outfits lining the little boutique, which were neither old-fashioned nor outdated, but instead comprised the latest designs, new and in-style. He could probably tell the shop was run efficiently by the gray-haired shopkeeper making the proverbial beeline for them. Would he be upset about his loss or accept it graciously?

The answer was clearly the latter when he turned to her and with a barely noticeable wink, whispered, "Verdict one to Kaitlyn Owens. But an appeal has yet to come."

She arched an eyebrow. "The ruling stands for now. Defendant owes plaintiff one hassle-free evening of obedience and adherence to whatever she has planned."

"Objection," he returned. "Nowhere in the agreement is there any mention of hassle-free. Which means I can do whatever I want..." His voice trailed off just as the shopkeeper reached them. With all traces of slyness vanished, he turned to the old lady with a smile that portrayed nothing but charm.

That scoundrel! The man planned everything perfectly, manipulating matters to get his way. But hassle-free or not, she still had the right to plan the evening. It would serve him right if she decided to spend it cleaning out the storage room. But no, she would not waste her evening in such a mundane manner. For now, she would stand back and enjoy watching Drake deal with Miss Ida, or more accurately, Miss Ida deal with Drake.

"Good morning, Miss Ida. My friend needs clothing for a week."

The old woman stopped in front of her newest customer and treated him to a long and thorough study. Miss Ida always gave clients a "looking over," whereby she silently noted and recorded all information necessary to produce the perfect wardrobe. Most people were taken aback by Miss Ida's brusque nature, but Drake's only outward sign of discomfort was a slight narrowing of the eyes.

"What type of clothes do you want?" The old lady spoke shortly, in a gruff voice powered by wisdom. It was the only question she ever asked her customers. Never accepting advice beyond it, she would quickly thwart any customer's attempt to plan his or her own wardrobe.

Drake responded in an equally smooth voice, "I would like several things. Perhaps a few gray polo shorts, khaki trousers, a couple of..."

"That's not what I asked," the old lady interrupted with a humph. "Who comes to a professional when they already know what they want?"

Drake raised an eyebrow, but didn't answer the obviously rhetorical question. Then his face relaxed, and his expression transformed into pure charm. "I'm not quite sure what you mean, ma'am, but you're the professional. Just tell me the information you need, and I'll be happy to provide."

Kaitlyn bit back a smile. Miss Ida would never fall for sly semantics. Silence loomed as the old lady studied Drake. "All right," she finally said in a voice more exasperated than angry. "We'll figure something out. Come along." She wrapped a wrinkled hand around his shoulder and led the willing prisoner away towards the back room. Kaitlyn was left behind, mouth agape, as she stared at the departing pair.

What just happened? Somehow Drake charmed the one person completely immune, or so she thought. Clearly, he was a better actor than she realized. If he could fool a sharp bird like Miss Ida, then perhaps they could actually convince Cynthia.

Her good humor restored, Kaitlyn idly perused the sale items as the minutes melted into each other. When Drake and Ida re-entered the room, all thoughts of clothing, Cynthia and everything else vanished.

Drake commandeered all attention.

His ensemble was neither designer nor formal, not unusual or standout. A simple yet stylish black silk shirt and tailored black pants, the clothing would have been unassuming on any other man, yet somehow on Drake it underwent an amazing transformation. From simple to splendid, from basic to beyond, the outfit and the man wearing it could be deemed nothing less than masterpieces.

There was nothing simple about the shirt as it stretched taut against rippling muscles, outlining strength it could not subdue. The dark absence of color added mystery, midnight black against smooth skin. The pants fit snuggly against his lean waist, perfectly coating long legs. He looked massive, powerful and authoritative, like an undercover agent defined by danger. No matter the cost, it belonged on their "accepted" list.

"Well?" Drake held out his arms. "What do you think?"

He looked like a Greek God. Or a double fudge sundae with whipped cream and a cherry on top. Better yet, a Greek God eating a double fudge sundae with whipped cream and a cherry on top.

Only she could never tell him that. She shrugged. "It'll do."

"We'll take it." His gaze remained pinned to her as he spoke to Miss Ida. The old lady clucked, no doubt already aware of her success. He strode toward the dressing room, stopped just before entering. "By the way, you can close your mouth now."

Kaitlyn clamped her mouth shut. Obviously, he was enjoying every moment of his effect on her. No doubt he would emerge again and again in equally sexy attire with equally sexy muscles and equally sexy drawls. And no matter her resolve, she would stare like she wanted to devour him.

What a disaster. How could she stand up to a guy she literally couldn't stop staring at? While licking her lips? And drooling?

In minutes that seemed like seconds, Drake emerged from the dressing room in yet another ogle-worthy outfit, this one casual, but no less stunning. It combined long khaki pants and a gray sweater to muscle-molding perfection, and made her want to run up, put her arms around him and see how soft that sweater really was.

And how hard the man was underneath.

This uncontrolled attraction was unacceptable. Perhaps it was time to start dating – a man nothing like Drake, of course. "That outfit's not too bad," she choked out. *Like the Atlantic Ocean wasn't too big.*

"Not too bad?" He raised an eyebrow. "Because the way you're looking at me…" He smiled wickedly.

"I've changed my mind. It's bad."

Drake laughed. "Bad, huh?"

"Terrible. I can barely look."

"You're determined not to like me, aren't you?"

"Of course not. I like you. A lot." *Crap. She hadn't planned to admit that.* "I mean, I like that you're here to help me with my... situation. I like you as much as any other guy." *What was she saying?* "Like my mailman." *She had completely lost her mind.* "Just take the damn outfit!"

He didn't say a word, just shook his head and retreated to the dressing room with far too smug a smile. This time, she didn't have to wait long for his return. Time seemingly stopped as he stepped into the light wearing a black button-down shirt and crisp jeans, powerful, capable and poised to conquer the world. The thin cloth did absolutely nothing to hide his stunning physique; instead it accentuated it, outlining long arms and tall and powerful legs. He looked like a cowboy from long ago, straight out of a western. "Cowboy Sexy" would be his motto if he had one.

"Cowboy what?"

Oh. My Goodness.

Had she spoken aloud?

Drake's eyes smoldered. "What did you say?"

"I didn't say anything."

His lips curved up. "Are you sure?"

"Absolutely."

"Well, if you're sure. But maybe you can help me with something. Do you think this outfit looks better with this button undone?" He released a black onyx button.

This was part of his plan for revenge. He was trying to drive her crazy. Kaitlyn gulped as a sliver of tanned muscle rippled in the v of the shirt. "I would say it's fine either way."

"Or maybe one more."

More smooth skin, more *powerful* muscle. This time she could only nod. And then shake her head. And then do something that was a mix of the two.

"Well, what about—"

"That's enough!" Could he see her struggle for control? His heated reaction said yes, as his eyes turned a smoldering gray. She drank in the sight of him, and the world between them disappeared. He looked as if he were ready to kiss her, a hungry predator hunting his prey. And the scary part was, she wouldn't stop him if he pounced.

She was considering pouncing herself.

"Why don't we talk about your outfit?"

She blinked at the unexpected comment. "I'm sorry?"

He examined her, from the very top of her head and going down very, very slowly. "I approve." The words were nonchalant, but hidden fire burned beneath them. He looked back up, stopped at the top of her outfit, where she had left one button undone.

The words emerged before she could stop them. "Should I undo another button?"

She covered her mouth with her hands. What had she said? If she undid another button, it would reveal far too much. Before he could respond, she choked out, "I'm kidding, of course." He stared, as if imagining what she did not reveal. "How about you try on another outfit?" she offered in a low voice.

Drake gave a curt nod. Only as he returned to the dressing room, his effect on her never lessened. *He's not for you, he's not for you, he's not for you.* Like a mantra, Kaitlyn repeated it again and again in her mind. Perhaps saying it out loud would help. "He's not for you."

"What did you say?"

Figures.

"I said you need to tie your shoe."

They both looked down at the same time. His shoes were tied. *Well, darn.*

"Actually, I heard what you said." He leaned back against the wall, causing the thin white shirt that outlined every muscle to stretch and become almost see-through. "It sounds like you're trying to convince yourself."

She cleared her throat, tearing her gaze away. "You already know the type of guy I want. Both in real life and for this part."

He stood up and the shirt loosened, as black jeans molded to muscular thighs. "I don't think you mean that."

Kaitlyn pulled herself up taller. "Excuse me?"

"I don't think you really want a man like that. Well, maybe for this role, but not in real life. You want a real man, even if you don't realize it."

"I never said I didn't want a real man. I just don't want a macho, aggressive, he-man of a–"

"I know, a tyrant," Drake broke in. "But you're a strong woman and you need a strong man."

"Why? To order me about?" That was exactly what she didn't want. "Tell me what to do?"

"Actually, I was thinking of something else."

Kaitlyn froze as a thousand images filled in the blanks. To touch her, kiss her, do *more* to her. She bit back a shiver as Drake's eyes turned as intense as the images seizing her mind. "Actually, I was going to say match you, but it seems like you've come up with your own conclusions."

"You don't know what I'm thinking," she snapped.

His challenging gaze belied every word, as he stayed still a moment more, before striding back to the dressing room. Just before the curtain closed, he called out, "Actually, I do."

No doubt.

For the next hour and a half, Drake tried on a dozen outfits, and she couldn't disguise her reaction a dozen times. Each was more attractive than the last, emphasizing Drake's gorgeous features and towering form. By the end of the fashion show, he had eight new looks ranging from casual to formal, and everything in between.

"This should be more than enough." Drake hefted four bags filled with clothing as they waited for Ida to ring up the order. "I found plenty of suitable clothing."

Kaitlyn had a different term for those tight jeans. "Yes, quite suitable."

"Four hundred and sixty-eight dollars." Miss Ida looked at her expectantly.

Four hundred and sixty-eight dollars? Kaitlyn stared at the elderly woman. Mentally calculating the droves of clothing he selected, not only was the price correct, but a fair deal. Yet that wouldn't appease her already strained budget. She hadn't a choice, of course, as she retrieved her wallet.

"Do you take credit cards?"

Kaitlyn looked up to find Drake holding a shining platinum card. "What are you doing?'

"Paying for the clothes." Drake handed the card to Miss Ida. "I can't believe how much I got for so little."

Almost $500 was little? "But aren't I responsible for all expenses?" As much as she didn't want to spend four hundred plus dollars, she had agreed to the terms of the contract, and she intended to honor them. "I don't want you paying for something that's my responsibility."

"This isn't your responsibility." Drake took his card back after Miss Ida swiped it. "I was supposed to come prepared, but the storm changed everything. Besides I could use the clothing."

His explanation sounded logical, but still something didn't ring true. How had the storm misplaced his clothes? Plus, how could an actor-for-hire afford to spend almost $500 without a second thought? "Hey, wait a second," Kaitlyn called as Drake signed the receipt, hunching over it as if hiding something. She peered around him. "Let's at least split it."

"Too late." Drake handed the receipt back to Miss Ida. "It's already done."

"I don't feel right about this." She took some bills out of her purse. "Here's part of it. I'll give you the rest later."

Drake looked down at the money, and, as if sensing he couldn't win this battle, pocketed it. "Ready to go?"

"Absolutely." Mollified, Kaitlyn turned back to the elderly shopkeeper. "Goodbye, Miss Ida. Thank you."

"Goodbye, Kaitlyn," the Miss Ida replied. "It was nice to meet you, Mr. Drake."

"Mr. Drake? No, Drake is his first n–" Kaitlyn turned to correct the woman, but Drake swiftly took her arm and led her out of the building.

"Come on. We have a lot to do."

"Wait a second." Kaitlyn strained to look back at the shop. "Why did she call you *Mr. Drake*?"

"Oh, you know, that's just how she talks. Adding Mr. or Miss to everyone's name. Don't you call her Miss Ida?"

"Well, yes, but…"

"Makes perfect sense. So anyways, where to now? Want to practice some more?"

"No! I mean, no, it's not necessary." Yet even as she protested, her body countered it was quite necessary, not to mention desirable, delicious and– She cleared her throat. Deep down, a small part recognized he had once again manipulated the conversation to his liking, but the rest was too caught up in the thought of *practice* to even notice.

"What about your apartment?" He changed the subject as they reached the Porsche. He opened the door for her, then folded his oversized body into the driver's seat. "Won't Cynthia find it odd it doesn't contain one picture of the two of us?"

Yes, they would. "I can't believe I didn't think of that," she admitted. "I told Cynthia about all our activities, and she's going to want the pictures to prove it. How are we going to get years of pictures in one afternoon?"

"Do you have a camera and a decent photo printer?" Drake turned the key in the ignition, revving the luxury car to life. He backed out of the spot.

"Yes, but how is that going to help?" she replied. "What do you want to do? Recreate every moment of our fictitious affair in photogenic glory?"

"Exactly."

Not exactly. "Greenfield is a small town. If we visit the local businesses, we'll run into dozens of people I know."

"That is a problem." He deftly maneuvered the car. "But there are lots of little towns not too far from here. Cynthia won't know if we took pictures at a local restaurant or one twenty miles away. We'll drive outside of Greenbeancasserole, far enough you shouldn't run into anyone you know. Will that work?"

Probably not, however he did not wait for a response before merging onto the main street. After reminding him the name of the town was *not* Greenbeancasserole, she protested the entire way, but he countered every single one. She even tried to convince him to stop at a quick photo studio to get professional photos, but he refused. Cynthia would be expecting photos of them actually doing things, he argued, not just one set of studio photos.

She gave up after they stopped at home to pick up the camera. They grabbed a quick meal of croissant sandwiches from her shop and several changes of clothing, which were neatly folded in the back seat. Once again they were on the road, in search of locales for their impromptu photo shoot. "So what do we do together?" Drake inquired. "Where to, boss?"

She rolled her eyes at the ironic term. This man liked being the boss, not following one. "You are my personal assistant." She thumped her chin. "Why don't we film you shining my shoes, dusting my perfume bottles, polishing the silverware, massaging my feet, stuff like that?"

He winced in feigned horror. "I do not shine shoes or dust perfume bottles, and I positively, absolutely do not polish silverware."

She couldn't stop a giggle, and his expression darkened further, although he wasn't truly angry. Suddenly he lightened, a devious expression replacing the horror.

Uh-oh.

"However–" He moved in. "I do massage feet. In addition, I have never gotten any complaints about my skills in massaging..."

"Don't you dare say it!" Kaitlyn hissed. Yet her body was already responding to the subtle hint his words promised. Unwanted images flooded her mind, of his hands on her body, blazing trails down her arms, her legs, her chest, *other* places. She closed her eyes against the visions, willed them to retreat. They remained in vivid glory.

"Backs," he finished gracefully. "I give great back massages. They are very good for relieving tension." He smiled wickedly. "You look a little flushed. What did you think I meant?"

"Absolutely nothing." The man was absolutely infuriating. "No pictures of you giving me a massage. Anywhere."

He didn't have the decency to appear the slightest bit abashed. "All right, although I must tell you, I have been rated as one of the top masseuses in–"

"Can we just drop the massage thing?" She didn't care how terse she sounded or how obvious his effect on her. "Can't we talk about something like colors or the weather or mud or something?"

The amusement in his eyes deepened, and she pressed on, "As for our activities, I told Cynthia you take me to romantic dinners, the movies, carnivals, parties, dancing, mini-golf..."

"Mini-golf?" He smiled and shook his head. "Only in Greengoat."

"Greenfield," she growled. "And remember, we're not in Greenfield anymore."

"Mini-golf it is." He winked. "Then to the movies, the carnival, the dancing clubs and all the romantic restaurants in town. Sound good?"

"Sounds impossible."

He grinned wider. "My dear, we are just getting started."

THE MINI-GOLF CENTER encompassed a charming one-story red brick building overlooking an eighteen-course grass field, flanked by flowers of magenta, lilac and yellow, along with miniature windmills, wooden bridges and copper statues of children at play. A tiny river flowed through the lush course, providing a delightful burbling backdrop. A brass sign stated it was owned by a fourth-generation local family, and judging by the number of cars, the center served as a hub of activity.

Kaitlyn gave Cameron a soft smile as he navigated the winding road leading to the parking lot. If only he could read the thoughts behind that beautiful sea-hued gaze. He'd pay all the profit from his last two settlements for just a peek of what churned there. Maybe then he'd be able to figure out why he couldn't get her out of his mind.

Was it because she was a challenge, not falling over him like the women he normally dated? Or was it because she wasn't judging him by the amount of money in his bank account? Was it because she saw the real him and not the façade he showed the world? If only it could be that simple, but a deeper connection loomed, something substantial, something elemental. She was just… different.

Normally women gushed at his gifts, but not Kaitlyn. He'd been forced to take her money in the store only to slip it back in her purse when she wasn't looking. And the funny thing was, she was the first person he wanted to shower with gifts in a long time.

Cameron inhaled the scent of gardenias and sunshine. Did she realize how much she affected him, or how deeply she invaded his senses? He tried to convince himself it was simple lust, yet it was a hopeless endeavor. Inexplicable feelings lurked, something he couldn't control, something he couldn't escape.

He was no longer certain he wanted to.

He pulled into a large parking lot, heralded by colorful flags and whimsical windmills. He tried to focus on the brightly painted buildings, to divert his thoughts from Kaitlyn. As usual, it didn't work.

"Have you ever played mini-golf, Mr. Alexander?"

"It's Mr. Alexander now?" He gave his most charming smile at Kaitlyn's teasing drawl. She returned it with her own. "Not since I was very, very young, Miss Owens."

"It's great fun. We'll actually have to play for real sometime." She winked.

"Absolutely," he returned in good humor, yet almost immediately he sobered, amidst unexpected dissatisfaction. They were unlikely to get the chance to experience this or any of their other dates for real.

He straightened. He had not gotten this far in life by simply accepting matters. If he wanted more time with her, he would make it. More than a week, more than a month, more than… forever.

Could he seriously be thinking in terms of something long-term with a woman he'd just met?

Yes, he was.

"Your Majesty."

"I'm sorry?" Cameron snapped his attention back to the delightful woman beside him. "What did you call me?"

"Not you." Her eyes sparkled with a dash of bemusement and a heaping of mischief. "We should have pet names for each other. I was suggesting what you could call me."

He bit back a laugh, but kept his face stern. "Oh, can I now?" He crossed his arms over his chest. "You would let me do that? I feel..."

"Honored?" she supplied.

"No..."

"Lucky?"

"I don't think that's it either."

"Wait, I got it. Forever thankful. That's how you're feeling."

He laughed. "You figured it out. I am deeply in your debt. How can I ever repay you?"

"Now you're getting a little corny." She skipped over a rock. "How about we just use first names?"

"You're the boss." And in a move that seemed perfectly natural, he looped his arm through hers, grateful when she did nothing to separate them. It was... perfect.

They entered the front gate together, strolling in contented silence. A charming and homemade operation, the center sported none of the mechanical wonders of the professional million-dollar complexes, yet it held a quaint magic that somehow transcended its big city siblings. No obnoxious plastic recreations cluttered the green, no neon signs bathed the world in artificial color and even the brook that babbled through the center of the course was natural. The center was built around it, not vice versa. It was... magical.

"This is nice." He pivoted all around. "As you probably

72

guessed, I'm not accustomed to small towns, but I can see why people fall in love with them."

Her cheeks beamed rosy with satisfaction. "They're great. Where do you usually spend your time?"

How to explain operating a billion-dollar business, traveling the world and running an international charity organization, especially when she believed he was an actor-for-hire? "I spend most of my time in big cities. That's usually where the job brings me." He pointed towards the line leading to the front. "Let's get some clubs and start building our album."

Curiosity tinted Kaitlyn's expression, even as she nodded. "Operation Get-Pictures-of-Dates-1-Through-50-in-Four-Hours-or-Less ready to commence. Let's go."

"THAT WAS THE QUICKEST DATE EVER," Kaitlyn commented half an hour later as she stretched her arms and legs, massaging well-used muscles. "Do you think we got enough pictures?"

"Definitely."

They'd jumped golf clubs first into the arduous task of securing photos to fool Cynthia. After paying for supplies, they asked other visitors to take pictures, and even played a few holes in between. They posed in action shots and simple ones, in sweet poses and playful hugs. Now they were preparing to move to the next destination.

That was, until giggles sounded from down the course.

Kaitlyn froze, her chest seizing in recognition. Surely, she could not be this unlucky. She pivoted slowly, froze at the sight of six laughing women who had just stepped onto the green. "Oh no."

Drake peered past her. "What's wrong?"

"This is not good. Really, really not good." She ducked

behind her would-be boyfriend, peeked out. The women were playing the first hole, and had yet to notice them. Once they did... disaster.

"Are you okay?"

"How will we get past them?" she hissed. "This is going to destroy everything!"

"What? Who are they?" He moved closer.

"No!" She grabbed his arm. Corded muscle rippled under her hands, and for a second all thoughts of Cynthia and discovery and the ruse disappeared. Drake grasped her shoulders like a true boyfriend would, eliciting the inescapable urge to delve closer. She licked cotton dry lips, glanced at his strong ones. His gaze was fathomless.

A breakout of feminine laughter, louder and closer, loosened the sensual hold. "The women," she whispered. "I know them. They visit the shop, and they know I don't have a boyfriend."

"They probably won't even notice me." His eyes slanted towards the women. "If they do, we can just say I'm a visiting friend."

"That's not how small towns work." With his warrior good looks, Drake Alexander would attract attention at the annual Greek God barbeque on Mt. Olympus. "They'll ask questions, make comments and then ask more questions. Then when my cousin comes, they'll make a point to visit, and the ruse will be up. I can't have six women trying to hit on my supposed boyfriend!"

A ghost of a smile lit his lips. "You think they'll hit on me?"

She responded automatically, "Of course, they'll hit on you. Any women in her right mind–" She stopped abruptly.

And he smiled like a cat who found a full fish tank and a fork. "Any women in her right mind..." he prompted.

She glared. "Any woman in her right mind would not finish that sentence."

The man had the gall to laugh. She grimaced, then stiffened as the women moved one hole closer. "This is a nightmare. If they see you, they're going to stay to chat. And if they stay to chat, they'll ask questions I don't have answers for. And if they ask questions I don't have answers for, they'll discover the truth. We need to get out of here before your acting career as my boyfriend comes to an abrupt end."

Drake instantly sobered, straightening to his full height. "Is there a way to reach the exit without passing them?"

"There's only one way out. We'll have to somehow pass them without being seen." She rubbed her forehead. "I don't think it's possible."

"Or get them to pass us," he said slowly.

"That won't work. They couldn't possibly miss seeing us." There were far too many of them. "There's no way out of this."

"We'll see about that."

Before she could interpret the cryptic reply, he swooped down...

And kissed her.

CHAPTER 6

ynthia who?
Pure bliss. Drake's lips were magic, as he brushed them against hers. He wrapped his arms around her back, his touch casting tingles on sensitized skin. She opened her mouth to sigh, and he pressed closer, touching tender lips. She could do nothing but accept the sensual pleasure.

Somewhere in the back of her mind, she realized she'd been turned around. Strong arms tightened, pulling her closer, melding her to him. The sound of feminine laughter sounded as if from miles away, and the rest of the world melted into nothingness under the onslaught of the kiss.

The sensual haze grew as Kaitlyn fought for control. She could not think beyond the kiss, could not pull away from the passion surrounding her. She never would have gained the ability if he hadn't slowly stopped moving, if he hadn't hesitantly pulled away. She heaved in deep breaths as she stared at him, until she realized… the path to the exit was clear.

Before she said a word, Drake put an arm around her shoulders. She did not protest as he drew her to the exit, past curious onlookers and grinning guests and into the sunny parking lot. They did not stop until they came to the car, or speak until safely inside.

"Did they see us?" she immediately asked.

He looked back at the entrance, but thankfully it stood empty. "I don't think so."

They had actually gotten away with it? "That was a great plan. People tend to see what they want to see, and since they know I don't have a boyfriend, they didn't recognize me."

His eyes flashed, questions and challenge tangling in their swirling depths. "A great plan," he echoed lowly. "Was that all it was?"

Yes. No. Not even a little. Yet if she admitted the truth… " Why else do you think I returned the kiss? I wanted it to be authentic."

He held the steering wheel, yet made no move to start the car. "That's the only reason you kissed me back?"

"Of course. Did you think I wanted you to kiss me?"

"Actually, that's exactly what I think."

Oh.

Somehow, he discovered the truth she could never voice. Yet it was unwise, risky and far too dangerous. She pressed forward. "Ready to go to the movie theater?"

For a moment, Drake didn't say anything. He then inclined his head, with challenge in his gaze. This conversation was not over.

He revved the engine, pulled out of the parking lot and glided onto the main road. They were silent as they drove, and twenty minutes later, they arrived at a tall building with movie star cut-outs and a giant marquee. They changed clothes and posed for shots, taking care not to stand in front of any of the current movie posters. After a few decent angles, they swiftly moved on.

They made a quick stop for refreshments and then raced

to the fairgrounds. Although no carnival lit the quiet grounds, a few permanent games stood by the main building. If were careful, Cynthia wouldn't realize they were at an empty park instead of a busy carnival. After setting the camera to timer, they posed in front of a game.

"Hold on a moment." Drake returned to the camera and shut off the timer. "This isn't going to work. What type of boyfriend am I going to look like if you're empty handed?"

"Empty handed?" Kaitlyn cocked an eyebrow. "What do you want me to do? Borrow a bunch of kids to pose next to us?"

He laughed. "Not that kind of empty-handed. Besides–" He grasped her hand. "I think we should wait a few years before children, don't you?"

Her heart stuttered to a stop, then slammed into the wall of her chest. It was a joke, a lighthearted comment in response to her own, yet somehow it elicited images, longings. She had to stay focused. "You're impossible." She swiped at him. He deftly caught her hand, and the world melted into the warm breeze. Dark emerald eyes ensnared her, wielded by the man who held her physically and mentally captive. As the air sizzled with a magnetic pull that defied the laws of physics, she moved closer.

This time there were no giggling women to hide from, no ruse to protect. This time it was all about desire. Their lips met and then…

Magic.

Borne of pure chemistry, the kiss consumed her. She moved without thought, powerless to resist the delectable man. Their lips tangled, soft and pliant, sensual caresses with delicious pressure. Shivers streaked throughout her body, sensitizing her skin and weakening her limbs. Time lost all meaning in the sweetness of the embrace.

Yet ever so slowly common sense forced its way into her

mind. She couldn't be with a man who stole all control, couldn't give up the independence she'd worked so hard to claim. Using all her strength, she finally pulled back. She touched swollen lips, stared at the man who did not appear unaffected. His breathing was labored, and his eyes mirrored her own hunger.

"Kaitlyn." He squeezed her hand.

"No." She edged back, broke contact. "This was a mistake."

"A mistake?" His expression was unreadable, his tone fathomless. Then he shook his head. "Yes, you're right. We cannot do this."

"Of course not." Kaitlyn paced, her body charged with waves of energy struggling to escape. "We do not belong together."

"How would it even work?" he asked. "You are a small-town entrepreneur…"

"And you're used to big cities. You travel, and I stay put. I'm your boss…"

"And I'll only be here a few days." He started to pace in a rhythm opposite of her. "I need someone who is quiet…"

"And mellow," she affirmed.

"Absolutely. Mellow. And you're not that. Neither am I. I need someone who agrees with me and knows it's best if I'm in control."

"Yes, in control. That's what I need to be," Kaitlyn agreed. "So you see, it's absolutely ridiculous for us to even consider being together."

"Because we're totally wrong for each other," he concluded.

"That's right."

"Still, I may just keep you."

"Wait, what?"

She didn't resist as he pulled her back into his arms, as they kissed in feverish urgency. Logical arguments and practical considerations dissipated into nothingness as he caressed her arms, smoothing her back and threading his hands through her hair. Passion ruled as Kaitlyn gave as much as she took, reveling in his strong and powerful touch. They were desperate for what only the other could provide.

She never wanted it to end. And yet somehow, reality managed to retake them, when the kiss finally ended minutes later. She blinked at the mirrored side of a game, the reflection showing a thoroughly kissed woman with flushed cheeks and sparkling eyes. What was happening to her?

She moved back, fought for strength. Gave the only appropriate reaction. "My goodness."

"I agree." He let out a low audible hiss. "You can't pretend that didn't happen."

"I can certainly try." Yet her voice trembled as she fought to regain control. She notched up her chin, drew a deep breath. "At least we'll be convincing for Cynthia."

There was so much more to say, yet a tangle of impossible feelings swamped her, with no name and no reasoning. She couldn't share how she felt. Not now, perhaps not ever. "We'd better get back to it. You know, the pictures." In the wake of the kiss, she had all but forgotten their important, time-sensitive task. "You were saying something about me being empty-handed."

He hesitated, and for a moment, she wasn't sure he would allow the change in subject. Yet then he straightened. "Be right back."

As Drake strode back to the car, she sank down on the soft grass, yet she couldn't decipher the madness that had commandeered logic and reason. She had asked for the kiss. Not pushed it away like she should have, not accepted it because she couldn't help it, but actually *initiated* it. What about him made her powerless to resist? "Cynthia will most certainly fall for the ruse," she mumbled, "because I'm starting to."

"What was that?" Drake returned, holding a very large, very fluffy teddy bear.

"Nothing!" She blinked at his offering. "What is that?"

"It's a prop, of course." He winked. "We actors use them all the time. Sometimes it's called evidence."

"What?"

"Never mind." He handed the stuffed animal to her. "You don't want Cynthia to think I can't win my lady a prize, do you?"

Kaitlyn shook her head. She didn't even want to know where he had gotten the toy. "You never stop surprising me."

"The feeling is mutual."

He set the timer on the camera and captured the moment. Yet in the flash, his earlier words returned:

I may just keep you.

FROM THE FAIRGROUNDS, Drake and Kaitlyn set off to the few dancing clubs near Greenfield. Although most were closed due to the early hour, they posed in front of them and got a few decent shots. Afterwards, they made the rounds at the local restaurants, asking curious patrons to snap photos. A few people commented that Drake looked familiar, although none could place him. When Kaitlyn remarked after the third incident, he shrugged and said he must have one of those faces. It seemed strange, yet another mysterious facet of Drake Alexander.

Two hours later, they had visited just about every restaurant in half a dozen towns and taken pictures of various places along the way. They snapped over a hundred photographs wearing eight outfits in countless "dates." With twilight near, the next date would be their last.

Drake took off his sunglasses as the sun's rays dimmed. "I don't know why I thought small towns had nothing to do."

"Shows how much you know about small towns." She lightened the words with a smile. They reached the car, and he opened the door for her. "The residents put a lot of time and effort into making this a special place to live."

"I can tell." He brought the vehicle to life and turned onto the road. "I'm enjoying this more than the big city."

"You seem surprised." She met his gaze. "You must travel a lot for work."

He hesitated. "That's true. My acting takes me all over the country, but not usually to places like this."

Why not? She bit back the question he was unlikely to answer, at least in a way that would elucidate matters. It was like that with a lot of things Drake said and did. He was like a puzzle, in which the pieces almost, but did not quite, fit.

Perhaps it was time to do a little investigating into Drake Alexander.

They drove in silence for a few minutes, before they arrived at a brightly lit building. He brought the car to a halt in a nearly full parking lot, then they disembarked and walked to a large brick building covered in green vines and cerulean flowers. The heavy scent of roses drifted on a gentle breeze, set to the music of nightbirds' song. Drake stopped at the small decorative sign hanging above the door. "You're kidding. You guys even have an ice-skating rink?"

"Sure do," Kaitlyn replied, "and right over there is the Killer Whale Aquarium."

His surprise was palpable as he pivoted. As he read the sign to *Jane's Sewing and Fabric*, he gave her a playful tickle. "You're kidding about that one."

"I admit it. But I got you." She dashed back from his touch, prouder than she ought to be. No doubt few people "got" Drake Alexander.

He laughed. "I'm not a very gullible person. Fooling me, if only for an instant, places you in rare company."

"Really?" She kept her voice light. "Do people often try to trick you?"

"Quite frequently."

Stranger and stranger. "But why? I would think it would be the other way around, with you being an actor and all."

He visibly stiffened, paused before answering, "I just find people are always trying to deceive you. That you must always be on guard."

"That's a shame."

"What?" He stopped walking. "Why would you say a thing like that?"

Kaitlyn stopped and turned around. "I would hate to face life believing most people were dishonest. I start by assuming the best in people, and they usually show it to me." She gestured to the town. "You seem surprised by all the amenities here. Is it because you didn't think a small town could afford all this business?"

"Actually yes." Drake nodded to a smiling couple walking out of the ice-skating center. "I've seen larger cities that couldn't carry half the business this place manages."

"Businesses survive here because everyone supports them." She plucked an old branch off a blooming rosebush. "When a tropical storm ravaged the general store, half the town came to pick up debris. When the movie complex almost closed due to tax increases, the local bank loaned them money on no collateral, and the landlord gave the owners extra time to pay. Things turned around, and they paid it all back. That's the way it is here. Good people, good business."

He stepped closer, grazing her arm. "Sounds like a pretty amazing place. In fact, there are quite a few amazing things here."

Her side tingled where he touched it, amidst the nearly irresistible urge to delve closer. She forced herself away from his touch. She couldn't afford to succumb to him or the impossible feelings he inspired. "Ready for our date?"

"Absolutely."

They paid the entrance fee and entered the ice-skating rink. The large facility was decorated in white and silver, featuring sparkly Styrofoam snowflakes and whimsical murals of winter scenes. Laughing children and adults in warm woolen sweaters careened this way and that, some graceful and some tumbling accidents on skates. Delighted shrieks filled the icy air.

They donned rental shoes and high stepped to the rink. Both were decent skaters, and they easily took to the ice, gliding in tune. They asked spectators along the sides to snap pictures, and within ten minutes had the necessary photographs. Drake slid to the carpet and reached down to unlace his shoes.

"Hold on a minute." Kaitlyn stopped him with a hand on his arm. A slightly naughty idea formed, somewhat devious, all fun. "Are you in the mood for a little friendly competition?"

"Friendly competition?" Drake raised an eyebrow. "Does this involve more practice?"

He was trying to get a rise out of her, but she wouldn't be affected. Well not that affected. All right, that affected, but she wouldn't show it. "Of course not. I always win *that* competition."

His grin widened. "I think we *both* win that competition. What then?"

She pointed to a white vinyl sign hanging above the concession stand.

"*Weekly Skating Competition*," he read. "A skating competition? You mean like figure skating?"

Kaitlyn laughed. "If I attempted a triple axel, out next date would be at the Greenfield Medical Center. No, they have a bunch of games, races, different things like that. You up for it?"

"It wouldn't be nice to show you up near your home-town." He winked. "Especially with you being my boss and all."

They both knew he didn't treat anyone like his boss. "I did win the right to plan tonight's date, remember? But if you're scared, I can plan something gentler like cloud watching, counting the stars, observing the grass sway in the wind–"

"Ma'am, I'm not scared of anything." His gaze turned seri-ous, and slightly wicked. "What I want I get."

Her breath hitched. Were they still discussing skating? "So do I."

"Then you're on."

They placed the camera in a locker and traveled to the front of the arena, where several dozen people had already gathered to partake in the weekly ice-skating competition she *often* joined. Had she forgotten to mention that to her competitor, or that she'd been dubbed local champion five years in a row? Although Greenfield wasn't the most competitive of places, she skated better than average and usually won the local ritual.

A small balding man with warm eyes and a bright smile came to the front of the crowd. Dressed in a t-shirt that read, "Ice skating isn't for the weak," he greeted most participants by name. The conversation quieted as he took out a small microphone.

"He's the owner," she whispered. "Bet you don't see too many business owners like that in the big city."

Drake smiled. "Sure you do, except most of them wear t-shirts that say 'Managing thousands of people isn't for the weak.'"

85

"Naturally," she teased. "And I assume you manage thousands of people."

"Of course, I do."

"Welcome, ladies and gentleman." The owner's voice reverberated through the cavernous hall. "It's time for our weekly ice-skating competition. There are seven games, with a first, second and third place in each. You get three points for winning first, two for second and one for third. The person with the most points at the end of the night wins. Is everybody ready?"

An enthusiastic cheer rose from the crowd, and the owner laughed. "Then let the games begin. But watch out – I spied a local champion in the back."

Kaitlyn smiled as the crowd cast glances her way. They were mostly acquaintances, so she didn't have to explain Drake to them. As for explaining them to Drake...

"What did he mean by that?" Drake's voice was calm, yet held the ever-present tinge of danger. This man missed nothing.

She blinked at him. "Mean by what?"

He drew himself taller, forcing Kaitlyn to tilt her head back to see him. Pure male force, his muscles stretched his clothing, flexing and releasing with unconcealed power. Green eyes sheened with intelligence, strength, and, for the moment, suspicion. Most people would not stand up to this man, yet she held as much strength as he. "Oh, that," she calmly remarked. "Did I forget to mention I win most of these competitions?" She tried to repress the smile... failed. "Oops."

He folded his arms across his chest. "Then I suppose I must also say oops."

She stilled. "What do you mean?"

"Did I forget to mention I was Ice Hockey MVP three years in a row when I was at Harvard?"

86

"Harvard?" Her employee was a Harvard graduate? As in one of the most prestigious – and expensive – schools in the country?

Who was this man?

A muscle ticked in Drake's jaw. "Community college. Harvard Community College – you know, the one in Idaho. You must have heard of it."

She narrowed her eyes.

He swiftly continued, "Seems like we got ourselves a little competition. Care to put a friendly wager on it?"

Harvard Community College? She shook her head to clear it. "Are you sure you want to do that, seeing as how I destroyed you the last bet?"

"A one-time occurrence, and I wouldn't say destroyed." He slanted his gaze. "I have an excellent winning percentage, and I don't intend to lose again. However, if you're scared..."

"Now you can stop right there. You're on, and I don't intend to lose, either." The manipulation was clear, yet she couldn't help herself. At the rink, they were preparing for the first event, signaling their time was up. "We have to hurry. What are the terms?"

"How about higher stakes?" he offered. "Take a real chance?" Her heart did a triple flip, as the danger notched higher. "If I win, I get what I really want, and if you win, you get what you really want."

A kiss. A thousand kisses. No, not just kisses.

Something real.

She swallowed. "What do you want?"

"More dates."

For a moment, something within her rejoiced. In the next, it crashed into cold reality. "I can't... we can't. It's impossible."

She pivoted away, yet Drake's murmured words stopped

her before she could escape. "I'm as serious as a big city lawyer."

More dates. Every moment they were together, it affected her to an extent she dared not explore. How much more could she handle before emotions delved too far? Then a voice whispered, they already had. "We've already admitted we're incompatible. You exasperate me, and I frustrate you. No offense, but you're not my type."

"And what is your type?" Vibrant eyes flashed. "It's certainly not that puppy dog you described, someone who will listen to your every whim, never question you. You're a strong woman, and you need a Rottweiler."

Heat engulfed her. "I know exactly what I want, Drake Alexander, and it's not an overbearing, domineering man. I hired you as an employee to deceive my cousin, and our relationship will stay purely professional."

"Purely professional?" he contested. "That's not how it seemed when *you* initiated that kiss at the fairgrounds."

"I made a mistake," she hissed, "but this has to stop now. Before… before…"

"Before what?" Drake challenged. "Before you realize something is there? Something neither of us expected, but can't pull away from? Whether this wager materializes or not, something *is* happening."

Sensual fire heated her blood. He was right. A connection had formed, no matter how she fought it. Of course, they would have to remain close, hug, touch and *kiss*, at least when Cynthia arrived. She couldn't escape it.

Couldn't escape him.

Was she really going to do this? She closed her eyes, opened them. "All right. I accept the wager. But here's the deal. If I win, you become the man I wanted in the first place. No more standing up to me, no more challenges."

He snorted.

"Hey," she warned. "You asked what I really wanted, and that's it. Take it or leave it."

He remained still for a moment. "Even though it's not what you *really* want, I'll take it. You've got yourself a deal." He stuck out his hand.

She hesitated. But it was too late to turn back without showing how much he affected her. She took his offering, and with a handshake, they sealed the deal.

Only if he won…

Could she handle something real?

CHAPTER 7

*C*ameron had sat in front row seats at the last Olympics. He befriended elite level athletes and held top tier tickets to the local sporting events. He himself played on numerous varsity level teams and had achieved black belts in several forms of martial arts, which he continued practicing to this day.

Yet nothing could compare to the anticipation of walking under neon lights and glittery plastic signs, hand in hand with the woman who was more enticing than a gold medal.

He'd admitted the truth to her. Not who he was, of course, but the connection he couldn't stop, the attraction that was far more than physical. Not only that, but he'd revealed his true goal and his willingness to chase it. He had no intention of losing this competition.

No intention of losing her.

They marched towards the rink, where the other partici-pants had already taken their positions and the announcer was explaining the rules. The first competition was freeze skate, a quasi-race in which the contestants had to stop skating when the official blew a whistle. Only those who came to a complete standstill would stay in the round. The game would repeat, eliminating skaters until only the winners remained.

Kaitlyn and Cameron both started out well, displaying their years of ice skating experience. They remained contenders when ten were left, stayed as the field narrowed to six and then four. Finally, only the two of them remained, and when the final whistle blew, Cameron wobbled just the slightest, and Kaitlyn won the event.

"Congratulations." Cameron took Kaitlyn's chilled fingers in his. The desire to warm, comfort and take care of her fired, and he rubbed her hands vigorously to create warmth. It created more than one type of heat as her cheeks turned pink. He leaned in, whispered, "The competition has only just begun. Next time, it's my turn to win."

And it was. In the following event, he took first while she took second. Thus set the rhythm of the competition. In each event, Kaitlyn and Cameron came in either first or second, alternating until the sixth event concluded, and they had scored an identical number of points. It came down to the last event, a six-lap race around the rink.

This was more stressful than the corporate espionage case Cameron fought a few years back. If he won, he would explore more of what was between them, but if he didn't win… well, that was simply unacceptable.

The duelists stood next to each other at the starting line. The whistle blew, and Cameron and Kaitlyn quickly outpaced the group, creating a comfortable lead ahead of the rest of the skaters. He was the more powerful of the two, but years of training had taught Kaitlyn how to move quickly on the ice. Although she would have been no match for him on land, on skates she had a chance.

They soared through one lap and then another and another, passing the slower skaters more than once. Finally, the prize came down to the final lap, yet it was still too close to call. Then... *a skater's nightmare.*

Just ahead of Kaitlyn, a teen skater sliced a turn too fast. He flailed his arms, his balance teetering on razor's edge as he overcorrected and overcompensated, careening the opposite way. The world sped like lightning as the skater succumbed to gravity, tumbling to the ice feet ahead of Kaitlyn. With no time to stop and no path of escape, she veered sharply to the left. The pressure proved too much for her ankle, and she plummeted to the frigid surface, the momentum of the race driving her forward like an out-of-control sleigh.

She *slammed* into the wall.

In an adrenaline-fueled haze, Cameron thundered towards Kaitlyn, as she lay motionless on the icy ground. The teen was already being helped up by his friends, laughing as he shook out his frost-covered hair, yet Kaitlyn was as still as the Arctic winter. Was she hurt? Did she have a concussion, a broken bone, worse? Terror seized every muscle as he reached her prone form. She was breathing, thank goodness, but her eyes were shut tight.

He touched her gently, did not move her in case something was broken. "Wake up," he commanded. "Talk to me. Tell me you're all right."

His heart hammered as he reached for his phone to call 911. Then her eyes flew open, bright and blue and lucid, and without a doubt the most beautiful vision he had ever seen.

"Drake." Her voice emerged hoarse. "I'm okay." She grasped his hand and squeezed tightly. "I just got the wind knocked out of me."

Even as his heart slowed, he loomed nearer. She said she was okay, but was she thinking rationally? Sometimes people suffered injuries they didn't feel. "We should still call for help. You should see a doctor or go to the emergency room. We could call for an ambulance and–"

"I'm fine." She gave a small smile. "I didn't even hit my head. No broken bones, but possibly a nice big bruise. I'm more concerned about losing the competition than the fall." She attempted a laugh.

"I could care less about the competition." He rubbed her cold arms. "You are all that matters."

Her smile faded. He hadn't meant to share that. Strong emotions emerged from hidden depths, the desire to possess, to protect, to keep her safe above all else. Raw and powerful, they demanded attention.

A doctor who had been skating arrived to check her out, and Cameron forced himself back. He also tried to force away the unexpected thoughts and unforeseen emotions, but they remained stubborn and present. So instead, he focused on the too-stubborn-for-her-own-good woman. When the doctor said to take her into the lobby so he could examine her, Drake scooped her up, carrying her off the ice under protest. Then he stood guard as the doctor examined her. It was not until the physician confirmed Kaitlyn's diagnosis of bruises, that the tension finally seeped away.

Kaitlyn gingerly sat down on the carpeted bench. "It's been an eventful day." She pulled off a skate and winced. "Let's just say it was falling down fun."

He did not laugh. He did not smile. He didn't even look up.

"Drake, what is it?" She reached out and placed a hand on his chest. The touch burned into him. "You've barely said a word since the race. It looked bad, but I'm all right."

He lifted his gaze, exhaled slowly. "You scared me when you fell, and when you closed your eyes..." He set his jaw. "I'm not accustomed to being out of control."

"It was scary for me too," she admitted, "but I'm fine. Even the doctor said so. And although it might not seem like it, I'm grateful for your concern. I even leaned something about Drake Alexander."

Despite his efforts, the sides of his lips tugged up. "What's that?"

"You're not as tyrannical, high-handed and despotic as I thought you were. Oh, don't get me wrong." She winked. "I'm not saying you aren't all of those things. Just less so than I imagined."

The smile broke through. "Thank you – I think. And you're not as imperious and bossy as I thought you were."

Kaitlyn laughed. "That's wonderful to hear." She turned to the ice rink, which had quieted. "We'd better go. Tomorrow will be a long day, and there's still plenty to do to prepare for Cynthia."

They rose to leave, but a call stopped them a moment later. They turned to see the proprietor racing towards them with two small blue ribbons. "Don't leave without these." He handed a ribbon to each Kaitlyn and Cameron. "Since neither of you scored in the last race, you tied for total points. Congratulations, you both won first place."

"First place. Well, how about that?" Cameron held the ribbon like an Olympic medal. "I guess neither of us won that bet."

Kaitlyn traced the satin ribbon. "You should be happy. Now you don't have to act like a puppy dog." She hesitated. "And we don't have to go on a real date."

He didn't say a word, as a thousand nameless emotions swirled. Instead, he turned and led her to the car, securing her with a hand on the small of her back. He relaxed as he closed the door, and she sat back on the soft fabric. It just felt right, her safe and sound in his care.

Their relationship had taken on a whole new meaning, more than a business agreement, more than a ruse.... just more. And suddenly there was far more to explore in this sleepy, small town.

THE RIDE HOME was filled with light conversation and last minute plans regarding Cynthia's arrival. Neither mentioned their earlier conversation, although it replayed a thousand times in Kaitlyn's mind. Again and again, she heard Drake say he was interested in more. Again and again, she told herself it was impossible.

Yet a traitorous voice whispered, was that entirely true? This man was not like she'd imagined. Unparalleled in strength and uncompromisingly clever, he was also undeniably kind, a facet he revealed in conversations of charities and good deeds, not by bragging, but accidentally sharing before changing the subject. He was still more tempting than an ice cream sundae, but she couldn't allow herself to indulge.

They went back over the details of her life and his role, most of which Drake thankfully remembered. Whether it would fool her cousin remained to be seen, but it would be nothing less than a worthy effort.

After what felt like an instant, they arrived home, Drake following close behind as she unlocked the door and let them in. He latched the deadbolt behind them. "You must be tired."

"Tired doesn't quite describe this level of exhaustion." She eased onto the living room sofa, stretching sore muscles. "We're just getting started. Tomorrow will be more of the same, and once my cousin gets here, it'll be even worse. I'm going to turn in early tonight."

"Sounds like a good idea. Want to take a shower?"

Um... what? "A shower?"

"Yeah."

With him? "Naked?"

"That's usually how it's done, yes."

Then yes, very much. Absolutely yes. Without a doubt, yes. We have a winner – please come to Kaitlyn to collect your prize! "Of course not!" she choked out. "Obviously there's been a miscommunication. I'm sorry if I gave you the wrong idea, but I'm not… that is, I don't think we should… you know."

Drake stared. "You know I meant alone, right?"

Well, crap. "Of course, I did! I mean, obviously."

His lips twitched. "I asked if you wanted to take a shower, because if you don't, I would. Alone. If that's all right with you?"

Of course, it wasn't all right. Why should he take a shower alone when she was here, all ready and willing? "Go ahead," she managed, covering her eyes with still chilled fingers. She heard rather than saw his departure, after a long hesitation. What was he thinking? No doubt he knew every wicked thought in her mind.

Unfortunately, the separation didn't dampen her imagination. Sound carried far in the small home, and unbidden images formed realistic scenes to accompany them. When he shut the bathroom door, her mind's eye saw a sexy promise gleaming in his eyes. The sounds of undressing drifted through the air – rustling fabric, shifting cloth, *unzippering*. Right now, he would be unbuttoning his shirt, taking away the thin layer that covered his muscular chest, his hands working in graceful moves. She could see his lean and powerful stomach, covered with definition and peppered with dark hair. Was anything sexier than Drake wearing low riding jeans and nothing more? *Yes!* her mind screamed as he began to remove his pants.

"I can't do this!" She sprang from the couch, grabbed her camera and busied herself printing out and arranging the day's photographs around the house, closing her mind to all thoughts of her too-masculine employee, with or *without* his clothes. But the shower faucet turned on, and her imagination again took control. Once more, she pictured the warrior, only now he was in the shower – glistening wet and *nude*. The water dripped down his gorgeous face and his powerful neck. Riveting down his lean stomach, all the way towards his...

A ringing sounded, and she gasped. "What am I doing?" She was supposed to be strong, the one woman in Greenfield immune to the gorgeous guy phenomenon. Or at least that's what she claimed. Drake shattered that rule, along with every other.

She picked up her cell phone, only it hadn't received a call. However, Drake's phone was plugged into a charger in the corner, its lit screen revealing the source of the ringing. What should she do? By the time she told him, it would transfer to voicemail. Of course, she shouldn't answer it – invasion of privacy and all.

Only...

Perhaps this was the opportunity she'd been waiting for, the chance to discover the truth behind the man of mystery. Besides, it had been a violation of privacy when he entered her bedroom that morning. Maybe he'd be glad she answered it, grateful even. With that hasty yet shaky logic, she snapped up the phone. "Hello?"

"Is Mr. Drake available?" The words were short, clipped and terse.

"*Mr. Drake*?" she replied slowly.

"Yes, Mr. Drake," the caller snapped. "Is he available?"

"No, I'm sorry, he's not."

"I should have known. You must be one of his secretaries."

One of his secretaries? Kaitlyn started to correct him, but the man just continued talking, "It figures. I'll leave a message. Do you have a pen and paper; this is going to be long?"

97

Confusion and suspicion weighed down her chest. Who was the caller, and why would he assume she was a secretary? Plus, why was he calling Drake "Mr. Drake," just as Miss Ida had? She grabbed for a pen and paper when the phone flew from her grasp. A powerful warrior loomed above her, wearing a thunderous expression – and not much else.

She. Was. Caught.

Drake was dripping wet, with only a towel to cover the necessary parts. Her throat dried at muscles upon muscles, power and strength she couldn't have imagined. Yet his face was the most striking, with a truth that shattered rational thought. This man was not a simple actor. He had to be more... so much more. She suspected it before, yet now it was as clear as his fury. Who was he?

Not a word pierced the silence. Finally, Drake turned and walked away, disappearing into the kitchen where she could hear none of the conversation. Moments later he was back, and the phone had disappeared. She stood tall as he came to face her, towering above her. The acute anger was gone, but his expression was no less intense. A weaker person may have backed away, but that had never been her style. She wanted the truth, and she wanted it now.

With all the courage she could muster, she boldly asked, "Why did that man call you Mr. Drake?"

He did not respond. He looked her up and down, and a lump suddenly formed in her throat. His body glistened in the light, powered by diamond droplets on a tanned torso. His arms held uncontrolled power, biceps and triceps proving physical strength as extraordinary as his mental abilities. His chest was defined and perfect, leading to a stomach that tapered down into a six-pack, reaching until the blasted towel took away her view. His chest rose and fell with controlled energy, but his face was the most beautiful of all, characterized by a strong jaw and piercing eyes. Right now, a storm filled them.

"Why did you answer my phone?" His voice was low and controlled, yet the calm tone belied his anger.

"It was ringing and there wasn't enough time to get you so…"

"It has voicemail," he interrupted. "You had no business answering my cell phone. Then you pretended to be my secretary."

"I never told him I was your secretary," she challenged. "He just assumed it. Which seems to be a mighty peculiar assumption for an actor-for-hire, don't you think?"

Drake's eyes flashed fire. "You were snooping around my business. Can you truthfully claim you answered my phone just to take a message?"

Lying would be useless with this man. "All right," she admitted. "I am curious about you, but all I did was answer the phone. He's the one who called you Mr. Drake and assumed I was your secretary. And you still haven't explained any of that!"

"So what?" He lifted his arms. "Nowhere in my contract does it say I have to completely reveal myself to you. You didn't hire me to divulge my personal history, but to be your pretend boyfriend."

"Which you haven't done at all!" Kaitlyn thundered. "My future boyfriend is going to be well-behaved and mild-mannered. He's going to be average sized, calm and agreeable. He'll be attentive, and he'll listen. In other words, not at all like you!"

"I don't think so, Kaitlyn." He leaned in, and the spicy scent of his nearly nude body enveloped her. She reacted with the heat of an erupting volcano. "That puppy dog you described is not what you need. You would chew him up and spit him out. You need a man."

She clenched her fists. "And that would be you, I suppose." She lifted her head, lying with every word, "You don't do anything for me."

"Oh yeah? Would you like to put a wager on that?"

He didn't wait for the terms.

He descended upon her, with all the passion of his fury. The kiss was bold and courageous, wild and daring, and designed to conquer. She fought to resist, commanding her muscles to move away and break the kiss, but they would not obey. Finally, when she had just about garnered the strength to pull back, he softened it to a gentle caress, a tender joining.

She was lost.

Passion splintered the world as Drake held her tight, as she wrapped her arms around his solid waist and dug her fingers into unrelenting strength. His chest was as hard as steel through the thin fabric of her silk blouse, molding against tender breasts. They pressed nearer and nearer, until no space at all separated them. But still it wasn't close enough.

It was as if no time at all had passed since their last kiss. He caressed her back, soothing tense muscles, eliciting soft sighs and gasping moans. His touch cast fiery heat, sensitizing a path on tingling skin. She traced his sculpted back, rejoicing in feminine delight when his breathing hitched.

She was melting like an ice cube in a furnace. All doubts disappeared, denials shattering under reality's truth. Her suspicions may return, along with regrets and reality, yet at this moment none of that mattered. The true man lurked behind the actor's mask, the real Drake who could not hide, as he kissed her with true abandon.

Ever so slowly the kiss ended, yet the desire burned no less. It was exciting and frightening, exuberating and disconcerting, to discover such a bond, an instinctual attraction that defied all logic. Questions burned in Drake's eyes, challenge, desire and indecision.

Yet for her, the path could be no other, and no matter the consequences, it heralded the right one. She wanted to make love to him, to share the promises in the depths of his eyes. This was a relationship that should not be, a tryst that could only last for days, but something in her demanded it. It was more than desire, more than attraction. "Make love to me."

His eyes darkened, turning as black as night. He could not conceal his desire nor the passionate male force that hungered for more. "There are things about me you don't understand."

No doubt, and yet she knew the true man. She placed a finger over his lips. "Do you want me?" she whispered.

He did not hesitate. "More than I've ever wanted anything."

Feminine satisfaction surged. "And I've never been so certain about anything in my life."

He gazed at her for a moment more. Then he moved forward, infiltrated her space, and *captured* her.

He lifted her into his arms, pressed against a steel chest. She gasped in surprise, even as elation slayed the shock, a sense of pure rightness as he carried her to the bedroom. Ever-so-gently he laid her upon the bed, and she leaned back upon the soft mattress, snuggling into the silky sateen sheets. He stayed still, gazing down at her until she opened her arms and beckoned him near.

Kaitlyn arched as he kneaded her skin with feather-light touches, worshipping every part of her. Desire consumed her, its strength undeniable and undefinable. His body was velvet-covered steel, a juxtaposition of power and strength, his hard masculinity the perfect foil to her soft femininity. She explored him, tracing corded muscle as she sought to uncover every secret.

Of course, he never relinquished his own investigation. As she grew braver, so did he, traversing her stomach to her arms and legs, her neck and face, closer and closer to the parts most aching for his touch. "You are magnificent," he murmured, stroking her with gentle yet firm movements, bathed in *possessiveness*. "As well as bold and brash and smart and sassy."

"I was about to say the same thing to you," she teased. She gasped as he brushed a nipple, and her voice melted into a whisper. "Make love to me."

"Yes ma'am." Drake kissed her lips, then touched a ripe breast, stealing her breath. Her nipples hardened as he encircled them, coaxing them to tiny beads. The need to be closer fired, to touch, to explore, to be one. As if he heard her silent plea, he shifted, unfastening the buttons on her shirt with a leisurely pace that nearly destroyed her. She shivered as he brushed aching breasts, unhooking the last of the clasps. His eyes darkened as he took in the swollen globes.

Heat filled her body, her soul, her world. A primitive force seized her, demanding her surrender. Struggling for rationality, she fingered the towel covering him. Drake's breath hitched at her touch, but still he kept his stoic control. She vowed to break that control before night's end.

Then he lowered the towel.

The oxygen disappeared from the world at her first full look at the true man. He was a masterpiece come to life, sheer perfection and flawless artistry. He flexed taut muscles, came closer. Then… he undressed *her*.

Kaitlyn shivered as he peeled back the lacy coverings, revealing tender skin under the sensual onslaught. Never had she felt so exposed, so glorious. His eyes dilated to diamond shards as he took in *everything*. "I can't believe it," he whispered. "You are even more stunning than I imagined."

No more words were necessary as he drew her closer.

With peppered kisses and bold hands, they explored each other, reveling in the sweetness of newfound intimacy. Kaitlyn moaned when he touched her most sensitive of spots, gasped when he stroked her tender core. Their bodies intertwined, she eagerly returned every touch. He jerked ever so slightly, betraying his stalwart control.

He stopped for the briefest of moments to don protection, and then nothing stood in their way. They moved against each other, faster and faster, bolder and bolder, until Kaitlyn could wait no longer. When he hesitated, silently asking the question, she opened for him. In one quick movement, he thrust into her, filling her completely. At his possessive strokes, she could only close her eyes and shudder, clutching him as he moved.

Passion took flight. It soared, leaving the earthly planes far behind. Kaitlyn fought for control, but could not contain the fire building within her. Lights twinkled before her until suddenly she could take no more.

She shattered.

She gasped at the same time he arched, amidst waves of passion that bore no words. Pure pleasure raced through her, in a world in which time meant nothing. She and Drake were no longer two, but one, united and whole, the only one that existed.

Time passed, and she descended back to Earth, back to her home and bed – and her lover. She pressed into him as her heartbeat finally slowed and she relaxed. Exhaustion reined, buoyed by a warmth and peace that was all Drake's. She lay nestled in his arms, curled into his body. Her lips curved into a soft smile, and although much needed to be said, she remained silent. No conversation was necessary on this perfect night. Tomorrow would bring clarity and reality, consequences and actions, but for now they both stayed still, content and at peace. With a soft sigh, she closed her eyes, succumbing to the sweetness of slumber...

And the man who remained a mystery.

CAMERON GATHERED Kaitlyn close as she slept, smiling like a cat with a belly full of milk. He kissed petal-soft cheeks, amidst a streak of hot possessiveness. She was where she belonged, in his bed and in his arms. He had never felt this fiercely protective, the thought of another man touching her almost too much to bear.

He had not been prepared for the wonder of their love-making, nor the tremendous connection they shared. Their physical connection was just part of it – something far stronger lurked. It was a peculiar sensation for him, a man who never lost control, surrendering to a woman who didn't even know his name.

Yet even if she didn't know the true facets of his life, somehow she understood more than the world who knew those details, right down to the cents lining his bank account. Long ago he erected a barrier to protect himself from the people who cared only about wealth and power, and yet somehow this slip of a candy store owner had burrowed her way past the facade to touch the real him.

And he had absolutely no idea what to do about it.

He inhaled air scented with chocolate and woman, the weight of confusion a heavy burden. His world was at best a precarious one; sooner or later Kaitlyn would discover the truth, and when she did, who knew how she would react? She had nearly discovered his identity today when his client called. He could scarcely believe the feelings that swept through him at the close call: anger, frustration and even fear, yet he hated lying to her. Even if the truth somehow stayed hidden, by design his position would last but days, and then he would be forced to return to his true life. A life without Kaitlyn.

No.

That was unacceptable. Impossible and intolerable, and he would not allow it. The attraction was more than physical, more than superficial. Indeed, every minute with her made him want a thousand more. Settling down next to his sleeping beauty, the future beckoned, eliciting a single question:

What if he simply refused to let her go?

KAITLYN FLOATED in a world of clouds and color, surrounded by peace, harmony and joy. That she was dreaming posed no secret, yet she felt no desire to emerge from its tender grasp, no pull to renter the world. She would stay forever if she could, encircled by perfection.

Yet a noise infiltrated the peace, a heavy banging that had no place in her dream. She sighed softly, wishing it out of existence, yet it only grew louder. Even as she resisted, the sound would not be denied. In a flash, the dream dissipated, fading away as reality intruded.

She expected disappointment, sadness and sorrow at the world's reemergence, and yet somehow she was as content and comfortable as in her dream. As the world traveled from blurry to focused, her senses sharpened to clarity, and she finally realized what was responsible for her joy – or rather who.

The man who had claimed her.

No word beyond claimed could describe the sensation of being held by the powerful man. The events of the previous night flashed, every word, every kiss, every touch. She turned to the source of her peace, pleasure and turmoil.

"Good morning," Drake intoned, his voice deep.

A thousand emotions swirled: *Joy. Concern. Delight. Fear. Happiness. Contentment.* It was a mélange that left her slightly unbalanced and more than a trifle dazed. With her cousin's impending arrival, she didn't have time to be either.

There were no regrets over making love to Drake. The joining had been spectacular and beyond, and she would not undo it. But now the consequences loomed, and she could no longer hide behind passion's curtain. Yet what were the consequences? The lovemaking had not satiated her lust; instead, her desire had only deepened, as if one night was not nearly enough. Could more than physical lust compel her emotions?

Yes.

The connection would not be denied, borne by a bond that transcended logic and reason. Emotions tangled with the potential to be extraordinary, yet it threatened this life she'd built. She mustn't succumb to raw emotion, no matter how strong. Only as she returned to the present and the man with smoldering eyes, every pledge departed, amidst a single question:

What if she took a chance?

What if she considered a true relationship with him? What if she reframed the circumstances as obstacles to be surmounted instead of impossible barriers? What if she listened to her heart?

She cleared her throat. Drake had waited patiently for a response, so now she quickly spoke, her voice emerging breathless, "Good morning."

Her lover smiled. *Her lover.* It sounded so foreign and yet so right. Forcing words through a tight throat, she spoke more authoritatively, "Did you sleep well?"

"I did." His gaze was fathomless. "Next to the most beautiful woman in the world."

Kaitlyn flushed. Sensitive cells came to attention as he

shifted, brushing against her in their lover's embrace. "And you?"

"Very well, thank you," she murmured. "I was having a very nice dream."

"Me too." He tightened his hold, and once again her body heated like firecrackers. How did he affect her with a simple movement? She had to get away from the powerful man and his intoxicating effect.

"Kaitlyn." His voice was like a lover's caress. She closed her eyes, retreating back to the night and the wonderous sensations it wrought. A part of her longed for a glorious encore, however Cynthia would soon arrive. She must prepare for her cousin, while somehow resisting her employee.

Yet as he traced a line down her neck, Goose bumps rose on tender skin, stealing wise intentions. Her body had already begun its treacherous betrayal and would not long withstand his sensual administrations. A moment's hesitation would mean hours more in his bed. "We should get up."

His smile was knowing as he released her from his embrace. "I'm getting to you, aren't I?"

Yes. "No."

"Are you sure about that?"

No. "Yes."

Kaitlyn slipped out of bed, strode to her closet and grabbed a pale pink silk robe. She cinched it about her waist, yet slowed as she tuned back to her lover. She had to say something lest he believe everything had changed. *Even if it had.* "What happened last night was amazing, but–"

"Stop." He rose out of bed. Sometime during the night he had donned his jeans, and now they rode low as he approached her, in the shadow of 6'2 of solid tanned muscle. He was an apex predator, all controlled power and stealthy movements. He gripped her hands in a light touch, holding her captive. "You cannot pretend last night didn't signify something. We must discuss it."

"There's nothing to talk about." She edged back, stopped by tether of his power. They had to return to a professional relationship before she lost all control. "We're physically compatible, but that doesn't mean our relationship has to change."

"Physically compatible?" he challenged. "This thing between us is far more than physical. I know it, and so do you. We can't just ignore it."

She notched up her chin. "We can and we will. I've already told you the type of man I'm interested in–"

"No matter how much you claim to want a puppy, it isn't true. There's something special between us." Drake's eyes darkened. "It will be explored."

Heat ignited her blood, but this time not from arousal. "How dare you! I will make my own decisions. We'll continue our professional relationship, and that's all."

"No." The words were calm, matter-of-fact, a simple statement of truth from a man accustomed to getting his way. "We don't have to continue intimacies, if that makes you uncomfortable, but I will not let you pretend this didn't happen."

Did he just suggest they stop intimacies? Of all the wretched, terrible, horrid ideas– *Focus!* "Did you just say no?" She glared. "You work for me. That means you have to listen to what I say."

"Then I quit."

Her mouth dried. "You can't quit." After all their hard work, he couldn't give up now. If he left, Cynthis would discover she'd made it all up. "You can't do that," she sputtered.

He shrugged. "Sure, I can."

"Are you blackmailing me?" she demanded. "Date me or I'll quit? I'll tell the agency. You'll lose your job."

He didn't appear the least bit concerned. "That's all right. I think it's time for a career change anyways."

"A career change?" Was he joking? Bluffing? Manipulating her to get his way? If so, it was working far too well–

A thunderous knocking shook the apartment and splintered her thoughts. She blinked as hazy memories resurfaced. "Banging… that's what woke me today."

"Me too." Drake frowned. Hammering pounded again, but unlike the soft noise of her dreams, this was far louder, more intrusive and definitely quite real. And it was coming from the front door.

"Who could that be–" She stopped, gasped. There was only person who would arrive at the crack of dawn without a moment's notice. Only one whose every move was to disrupt and dismay. Only one who could pick the perfect time to force her surrender to Drake's blackmail.

"Cynthia."

CHAPTER 8

"Cynthia?" Drake stared. "She wasn't supposed to arrive until tonight."

"She always liked surprises." Kaitlyn rubbed sweaty hands against an ice-cold face, a painful juxtaposition of sweltering and freezing, mired in perfect chaos. This couldn't be happening. It was too soon – they'd never be able to pull off the ruse without another day to prepare. "Maybe we can pretend we're not home."

"Nonsense. This is perfect." Before she could protest, he straightened, smoothed himself down and... stepped to the door.

Oh no. She raced in front of him. "What are you doing?" Her demand tangled with the intensifying banging. It was the antithesis of perfect, a disaster with the power to destroy all.

His mild expression belied the calamity. "Now you have to agree to my proposal."

Why that little–

She glared.

He winked.

She growled.

He grinned.

"You underhanded, sly, devious and... and..."

"Successful man?" he supplied.

"Ugh!" She gripped his naked arms, totally ignored the hard muscle underneath (That was a lie). "You can't do this."

He leaned down, his hot breath fanning her neck, eliciting more urges she totally ignored (That was another lie). If she moved just a little closer–

"Is that a yes?" he breathed.

She closed heavy eyes, opened them to a predator poised for victory. "Fine!"

He ducked out of the room before she could say another word. She ran after him, nearly slamming into his colossal form as he reached the door. She braced against the broad muscles of his back, as the jeans slid lower. He pulled them up (quite inconsiderate), turned the lock and...

"Wait!" She grabbed his hand. "You can't answer the door like that."

"Why not?" Drake kept his hand on the handle, but ceased his motion. "What's the matter?"

"It's inappropriate." She gestured to his scant ensemble, expansive chest, barely-covered *everything*. "You're not decent."

He shrugged. "It's not decent showing up this time in the morning. Besides, this is the perfect cover for our ruse. What else would two lovers do but spend the entire night making love? If we hadn't done it for real, we probably would have made it up. Relax," he soothed. "It's not as if I'm meeting your parents."

She exhaled. Meeting Cynthia after a night of passionate lovemaking would be a convincing first act to the play. Commanding herself to calm, she straightened. The stage fright would have to wait. It was show time. "All right. I'm ready."

With an approving smile, Drake nodded. Time ticked in slow motion as he turned the handle, then slowly, slowly, slowly opened the front door, revealing the expected surprise. Cynthia wore an unpleasant smile and a chic banana pantsuit that would have been more appropriate at a party cruise than an early morning visit to her cousin. Ostentatious and gaudy, with an air of malevolent triumph, it was not nearly as blinding as the sight behind her.

For she was not alone.

The entirety of Kaitlyn's immediate family – her mother, father and two brothers – stood like a family portrait, eyes wide as they took in Drake, or more accurately *nearly-naked* Drake. Her mother parted her lips, her father folded his arms and her brothers clenched their fists. No one spoke, and no one moved. That is, not until Kaitlyn did the only logical action.

She slammed the door shut.

"Kaitlyn!"

"Don't touch it!" She grabbed Drake's hand before he could grasp the knob, threading her fingers through his much larger ones. Her heart thundered against her chest, shaking her ribs and stealing her breath. "My family was there. They all saw you. What must they think? What will I tell them?" She was rambling, but she couldn't stop. The oxygen had disappeared from the room. "There's no way to fix this."

"It's going to be all right." He placed a firm hand on her shoulder. The touch was warm and possessive, and unexpectantly comforting. "We'll figure it out."

"How?" She grasped him tighter. He didn't have the decency to flinch. "This is my family. People I actually care about." She shuddered, threading air through a tight throat. "What am I going to do?" she rasped.

"All will be well." He edged closer, rubbing up and down

her arms, even now eliciting Goose bumps. "We will follow the plan and pretend we're a couple. It's not that far from the truth."

Her breath hitched at the presumption, yet somehow a denial wouldn't form. She pressed forward, "I don't mind lying to Cynthia, but how can I deceive my parents? Only how can I admit the truth?"

Drake's gaze focused as a sharp knock shook the door. "It's your decision. We can stop now and admit you made it up. Or we can proceed for a few days. Remember, it won't be completely lying since there *is* something between us."

What calamity to respond to first: the decision about her family or his assuming statement? The next knock, the loudest one yet, signaled only seconds to decide before her brothers broke down the door.

Then, suddenly, the path became clear. She would go through with it. Although her family might eventually learn of her deception, they would never stop meddling if they discovered the truth now. "Let's do this."

Admiration tinted Drake's eyes. "Sounds good, boss." He did not hesitate as he flung open the door to a crowd of stunned relatives, focused on the man who commanded all attention. Her mother stood up front, pretty and petite, her intelligent blue eyes flush with curiosity and care. Next to her, Kaitlyn's well-built father loomed, glaring fierce protectiveness. Her two older brothers, larger than her father and even more protective, stood on either side, wearing dark trousers and shirts that showed off the muscles they'd happily use to protect their little sister.

In the middle of it all stood Cynthia, of average height, with tight black curls, deep brown eyes and a small, upturned nose, brimming with smug satisfaction barely hidden behind false concern. She was the first to speak. "What in the world is going on here?"

Kaitlyn opened her mouth, poised with a long and imaginative excuse, but Drake was quicker. "Cynthia." As the woman froze in astonishment, he smiled with his signature charm. "I'm so glad to finally meet you. This is a wonderful surprise."

"A surprise is right." Her father's expression darkened to a stormy gray. "We weren't expecting to get the door slammed on us."

Kaitlyn stiffened like a fresh corpse. Why had she thought this would work? Perhaps it was best if she came clean now and avoided any further humiliation.

Drake frowned, as if sensing her wavering conviction. As her family shuffled in, he leaned down and whispered, "At least we know who's stronger now."

She narrowed her eyes.

"Since you've obviously given up, it proves I'm more powerful."

His attempt at manipulation was obvious, yet anger brought newfound conviction. Perhaps the plan had a spark of life left after all. "Mom, Dad, everyone, I'd like you to meet Drake Alexander, my boyfriend."

It was as if someone pressed the pause button on reality. All movement stilled, her family stared and silence ruled. A hundred messages cut the tension thick in the air, as everyone regarded her would be paramour.

Well, that could have gone better.

Drake hit resume. "This must come as a surprise. We wanted to wait until we were sure before we told you."

"Sure of what?" Her father's eagle-sharp gaze speared Drake. "Sure you could afford a shirt?"

Drake wasn't at all disconcerted. "My apologies, sir. I just came out of bed and wasn't expecting guests. I meant sure Kaitlyn and I were serious about the relationship." He focused his world-class smolder directly on her, engulfing her in fiery heat. How could he seem so sincere, so real?

What if it wasn't pretend?

"We didn't want raise your hopes," Drake continued mildly, as if he wasn't ravaging her senses. "You know how independent Kaitlyn is."

"Don't I ever," her father grumbled. "How did you meet my daughter?"

Before Drake could reply, her mother broke in, "Stop interrogating the man, George. Any friend of our daughter is a friend of ours." She held out her hand. "It's a pleasure to meet you, Drake. I'm Judy Owens, Kaitlyn's mother."

"I'm Craig." The eldest of her two brothers inclined his head. "I'm glad to meet you and eager to find out more." His protective expression hinted at the type of details he meant, yet still his tone was softer.

Kaitlyn took a deep breath. So far so good. Her family appeared to accept him, at least for now, and had yet to call the FBI, CIA or mafia. If they could put on a convincing performance, they had a chance of making this work.

"I'm Jesse." Her dark-haired brother stepped forward and shook Drake's hand in a strong grasp. "I'm a second-degree black belt."

"Jesse!" Kaitlyn admonished.

"Just sharing, sis." Her brother shrugged.

Drake chuckled, clearly not intimidated. "That's okay. I'm actually a third-degree black belt. Perhaps we could exchange techniques sometime."

Kaitlyn stared at Drake. He couldn't possibly be an actual martial arts expert – or could he? It was a stark reminder of how little she actually knew about this man.

"I understand what you're implying." Drake smiled affably at Jesse. "But don't worry. I take care of my Kaitlyn."

She stiffened. "I don't need to be taken care of."

Correcting him wasn't conducive to their act, yet she couldn't stop herself. She was a strong woman.

Somehow Drake's brazen assumption didn't seem to bother Jesse, as he grasped her in a warm embrace. "Everyone could use a little help sometimes. Of course, you'll always be our little sister, and we are *always* here for you." He lowered his voice to a whisper. "Everything okay?"

"I'm fine," Kaitlyn responded quietly. Her brother nodded, yet doubts clouded his eyes. With a genius IQ, he would be the most difficult to convince.

"My name is George." Kaitlyn's father once again took control, with only a slightly less accusatory tone. "I am sorry for barging in like this. It was a shock to hear of your relationship, especially from Cynthia." He turned to his daughter. "Why didn't you say anything?"

The spotlight was on her, and it would have to be an award-winning performance. As any good actor would say, the best act incorporated as much of the truth as possible. "I'm sorry, everyone. As we've already established, I'm pretty independent."

Six heads nodded in instant agreement. "Never wanted help with anything," her father said gruffly. "That's how Kaitlyn was since the day she could talk."

She had definitely picked the right angle. "Exactly. I didn't plot to keep this from you. At first, there was nothing to tell. Drake came to town, and I hired him to be my personal assistant. As you know, the store has been getting bigger, and I needed a little help. And for a while that's all it was, a business relationship."

"But then things changed," Craig interjected.

"Yes. Everything changed." Kaitlyn hesitated, at the tale that mirrored reality. First a business relationship, then more. She pressed on, "Our relationship progressed to something beyond business."

"Why didn't you share this amazing relationship with us?" her mother broke in. "For all this to happen, and not a word?"

Guilt assailed Kaitlyn. Her mother's voice was filled with hurt, in stark contrast to Cynthia's mischievous yet controlled expression. She had yet to contribute to the conversation, but suspicion loomed dark in her frigid eyes. No doubt she would have much to say later.

It was too late to turn back. "Time just passed so quickly, and then I didn't know how to tell you. I was going to say something very, very soon." She held out both hands. "And that's the entire story. I'm sorry, guys – I hope you can forgive me."

There it was. The concluding sentence, the final bow and curtains closed. Kaitlyn held her breath, awaiting the audience's reaction.

"Unbelievable."

She closed her eyes. "Dad..."

"Our little girl is finally in a serious relationship. It's about time."

Kaitlyn barely held in the gasp. It *had* worked.

"This is wonderful!" Her mom embraced her, then gave Drake a quick hug. Each of her brothers followed suit, although with handshakes and not hugs. Yet guilt tempered her joy. She had lied to the people she loved most. The deception would be temporary, and soon she would explain everything and beg their forgiveness. Hopefully, Cynthia would remain in the dark forever.

Her cousin had been uncharacteristically silent, but now she broke it. "I'm so happy for you. Tell me, has your relationship changed his employment as your personal assistant?"

Kaitlyn subdued a grin. Her unwanted guest had inadvertently stumbled on the one subject she relished. "Not in the slightest. Drake likes being my personal assistant. He says it's his calling."

Drake visibly tightened. She happily ignored it. "Between me and you… and you… and you… and you… and you…" She regarded each of her relatives in turn. "He has a bit of a subservient personality." She winked.

Drake set his jaw, but then… mischief sparked. *Uh-oh.* "I think my Kaitlyn is a little confused. She definitely needs someone to guide her. Can you imagine the crazy things she'd do if I wasn't here?"

Actually, she only started doing crazy things *after* he arrived. "Men get such silly ideas sometimes, don't they?" She patted his rock-solid chest. He covered her hand with his own, entrapping her against pure steel. *Oh my.*

She swallowed, turned to her father. Time for a distraction. "It's just so wonderful to see you. How long are you staying?"

"Just a few days. I have to get back to work."

She exhaled relief. Normally, she loved her family's visits, yet for this trip, the shorter the better. A few days she could handle, and then everyone would leave, and life would go back to normal. Only dissatisfaction tautened limbs, amidst an undeniable truth:

Drake would leave, too.

"We wouldn't want to impose on you for more than a few days."

That was nice. They really were very considerate and– She froze. "What do you mean… impose?"

"You don't have a lot of space here, and with Drake, it'll be very tight. You shouldn't feel like you're being watched for too long." Her mom laughed lightly.

Oh. My. Goodness. "Of course not." She turned to Drake. "Honey, a private word?"

"Sure." Drake grasped her hand "We'll be right back."

Everyone smiled and waved as he led her to the bedroom. "Take your time," her father called after them. "We'll be unloading the air mattresses from the car."

Unloading the air mattresses? She cringed as she closed the door behind them, but did not speak while Drake pulled on a t-shirt. She frowned as it covered his chest. Really, after all the trouble he'd been, the least he could do was provide an interesting view.

He looked up. "Did you say something?

Um, had she said that aloud? "No."

"Are you certain, because I thought you said something about a view–" He grinned, but his expression soon melted into soberness. "Are you all right?" he asked in a soft voice.

"Of course." Yet she couldn't look at him as she strode to the closet and grabbed a rose-colored sundress. "I'm going to change."

She took a step toward the bathroom, stopped at his words. "Is that really necessary after…"

Her gaze inadvertently drifted to the bed. After what she'd seen – what they'd done – leaving to change was point-less. Still, she averted her eyes as she swiftly slipped off the nightgown and donned the dress. Neither mentioned her flushed skin or his darkening eyes.

When she finished, he was all serious. "Tell me they were speaking figuratively when they said they were staying here. Tell me *here* meant the town of Greeniesville."

"That's Greenfield." She grimaced. "And they meant here, in my house. In my family, one person's home is everyone's home. Normally, I don't mind hosting, but just this once, I wish they'd rented a hotel room."

"Can't you ask them to stay somewhere else?"

She snorted. "Not if I want our ruse to have a chance. They'd know something was off." She sank down on the bed.

How had things gotten so complicated? "What are we going to do?"

He sat next to her, placing his hands on her shoulders. "We're going to continue with the plan." With gentle yet firm movements, he massaged her, smoothing sensitive flesh and melting tense muscles. A protest danced on her lips, yet instead she sighed, arching into his administrations. Perhaps they could lock themselves in the room and escape her family altogether.

He leaned closer, casting his woodsy scent over here. "It's all right they're staying here," he murmured. "Getting closer is part of our deal anyways."

Kaitlyn shivered as her control faltered. "Our relationship will soon be over." Yet the words were light, the tone breathless. They didn't even convince *her*.

Across the room, the knob to the bedroom door turned. Even as she tensed, Drake leaned closer and closer. "Oh no, my little firecracker, it has only just begun."

He matched his lips to hers.

CHAPTER 9

*I*t was like opening Pandora's box.

Kaitlyn kissed Drake with unrestrained fervor, pressing into a rock hard chest, filled with power. The kiss was sweet and savory, as Drake captured her once more in his powerful hold, surrounding her with pure muscle-bound strength. *Delicious.*

In the background, a throat cleared, followed by a soft cough. A thousand consequences loomed, yet still Kaitlyn could not retreat. It finally ended as Drake released her, yet it seemed more a beginning than a conclusion, a promise of more to come. Yet not now, when her family stood at the door with a hundred expressions of surprise, embarrassment and *delight.*

Craig finally broke the silence. "I must say, sis, I was skeptical at first, but now..."

A slow blush heated her cheeks, yet it was Drake who responded, "Some things just can't be hidden."

She looked up sharply. Her employee matched her gaze, his eyes dark, mysterious. Was he role-playing or sharing a hidden message only for her? The questions required privacy, a commodity no longer available.

"We didn't mean to intrude." Her father's voice held neither approval nor disapproval. "You have a visitor."

"Thanks, Dad." She held her head high as she walked from the room. With her luck, it would be her entire extended family, along with the local news to do an exposé on fake boyfriends. When she opened the door to Allison, she exhaled in relief, which died a second later at the concern etched in her friend's features.

"I tried to fix this on my own, but everything imploded, and I don't know what to do." Allison's words blended together in a single breath, as she stumbled into the apartment. The normally unflappable woman was beyond disheveled, small wisps of hair escaping a messy bun, flour coating not only the fuchsia apron, but the sunshine yellow dress underneath. She looked (and smelled) like a cupcake explosion. "Remember that big order you have for today?"

Kaitlyn stiffened. The order was her largest to date, nearly a thousand dollars worth of baked goods for an out-of-town party. The customer was from an influential family and promised scores of business if all went well. "It shouldn't be too much. We already finished the prep work, and I pre-made the dough. My employees will spend the entire day helping you finish."

"Except the refrigerator had a meltdown this morning – literally." Like a flour fairy, Allison fluttered back and forth. "The handyman was able to fix it, but everything is sort of ruined, and by that, I mean completely and utterly ruined. Then three of your employees called in sick at the last minute – apparently they all got food poisoning from the same takeout yesterday. You only have one employee coming in, and she'll need to work the shop."

Yes, she would. A thousand options flashed, yet none were

plausible in the time they had left. Kaitlyn slumped at the undeniable reality. "I'll call the client and tell them we won't be able to complete the order. The event is today, but maybe if we explain…"

"Absolutely not."

Kaitlyn pivoted to find Drake's powerful form looming above her. "What?"

"It's corporate sabotage to abandon an order the day of a party. They'll tell everyone what happened, before praising the competing bakery they used after you didn't deliver."

No doubt. After all her hard work, this could decimate her reputation. Yet what choice did she have? "This is really none of your concern…"

"Not his concern? He's your personal assistant."

Cynthia's voice chilled her into silence. Drake was indeed her pretend personal assistant, which would make it very much his business, but this was real life. Her business and her life. "Of course, he is." She forced a smile. "I meant, there's nothing to do. The preparations have been ruined." She exhaled lowly, as her dream turned into a nightmare. "This could have meant a lot for my business."

"Which is why we need to deliver the order." Drake rubbed his hands together. "What time are they picking it up?'

"Five o'clock. It may seem like a long time, but I spent hours on the ruined goods. There's far too much to complete one day. Even if I started this minute, I couldn't possibly finish."

"Which is why you have a personal assistant." Drake inclined his head. "And a friend who is willing to help." He pointed to Allison. "If we start now, will we be able to finish?"

She bit her lip, considered the tasks to redo the order. It would be tight, but if she postponed most of her daily activities, they just may be able to do it. And the frosting on the cake – she wouldn't have to spend the entire day with her family.

"Nonsense."

Kaitlyn's smile wavered as she turned to her father. "Dad–"

"How can we sightsee while you frantically work to salvage your business?" He gestured to the rest of the family, as they nodded. "We'd like to help, too."

Kaitlyn turned a sideways glance at Drake, who gave a barely visible shrug. It had seemed the perfect way to separate the family, and now they would be closer than ever. Yet there was no logical reason to refuse his offer, and it would increase the likelihood of finishing in time.

"All right." Drake nodded. "Let's get started. Everyone down to the shop." It was an order, but no one seemed to mind the directive from the natural leader. A worthy skill for a performer, but far more valuable in other, higher positions. Once more the question surfaced, of why a man with so many skills would be an actor-for-hire.

"Coming?" Drake turned back to Kaitlyn. The rest of the family had descended the stairway, and for a brief moment they had privacy. A lock of hair fell across his forehead, and she resisted the urge to smooth it back.

"Are you really an actor?" The words emerged before she could stop them, borne of suspicions from the moment he pummeled through the door that dark stormy night until his recent behavior and every mysterious action in between. With every moment, new doubts soared.

His eyes widened in surprise – from the question or because she had discovered the truth? His usual stalwart control returned a moment later. "I can honestly say I'm acting right now." He pivoted toward the stairs.

It took a moment before the words hit. "Wait. What aren't you honest about?"

Before she could ask again, he disappeared down the stairwell. She ran down the steps, two at a time, until she reached the bottom. Racing through the kitchen door, she nearly tumbled into Drake, and only avoided falling by clutching his muscular form. Desire flooded her, and somehow she forced herself back. She spoke before he could utter a word, "Have you been untruthful?"

This time he heard her.

As did Allison, Cynthia, her mother, her father and her brothers.

Drake's expression transformed in an instant. "Honey, I know you're upset about the order, but let's not argue. I am always truthful with you." His tone was calm, but an edge belied the benign words. Like spectators at a sports game, her family looked from him to her and back again.

A thousand questions blazed, yet in her family's presence she could ask none. "I know you are." She forced a smile. "You're the best. So..." Kaitlyn turned away from her would-be employee/hired actor/real lover before anyone could doubt their sincerity – or her sanity. "Is everyone ready to work?"

"Bring on the chocolate," her elder brother grinned with good-natured charm.

Everyone was ready to help, with the expected exception of Cynthia. At least it would be fun putting the unrepentant troublemaker to work. "Mom, Dad, I'd like you to help Allison prepare the croissants. We need a truckload of them, all types, shapes and sizes." She turned to her brothers. "Do you think you can manage to make fudge without eating the results?"

"No," they replied in unison.

"Well, try." She laughed, pointing them in the direction of the refrigerator. "Drake, you can help me with the cookies. Cynthia, I'm afraid I don't have any cooking tasks for you."

125

The distasteful woman's upturned nose wrinkled in fake disappointment. "Oh well, I so wanted to help. I guess I'll just have to supervise."

Kaitlyn smiled. "Well, since you really want to help, there is one thing…."

Maybe this wasn't going to be such a bad day after all.

✹

AS ALWAYS, Drake stole Kaitlyn's attention the moment she entered the kitchen. He stood at the counter, working the dough into little stars and moons with his large, capable hands. His expression was pensive, and for once he didn't notice when she came right next to him. "What world are you on?" He started, and she reveled in the rare opportunity to take charge. "You really were in space."

"Apparently." He straightened his shirt, but then his lips curved. "Want to know what we were doing on this other world?"

Oh yes. "Nope."

"Are you sure? It seemed like you were having a good time. A great time, even. In my dreams you were…"

"Don't you dare…" Kaitlyn warned.

"Washing my car."

"I'm not going to honor that with a response," she huffed, barely hiding the smile. "So you'll never guess what Cynthia is doing."

He chuckled. "You're as bad as you claim I am."

"It's not my fault the only job left was cleaning the mess from the fridge mishap." She grinned. "I thought Cynthia was going to pour a bag of flour over my head, but she wouldn't dare refuse in front of my family."

"You'd make a good lawyer. Brains and the body of a goddess. Who could resist?" He stepped a little closer. "If I seem distracted, it's because you're irresistible." Closer still, his voice dropped to a murmur. "But as beautiful as your body is, your mind is the most tempting of all."

She shivered, fought the urge to toss him over her shoulder, take him upstairs and have *her* wicked way with him. His eyes darkened, as he splintered her thoughts. A mere breath away, he trapped her under his gaze, and her traitorous mind crafted more images.

Chocolate was involved.

She had to say something before she did something she would (or would not) regret. "That's it, you're definitely cleaning out the freezer."

He laughed. "That, my dear, was a classic statement of misdirection."

"Oh? Well, I–"

"Would you guys quit teasing each other and start working?" a rough voice interrupted. They couldn't see her father, but apparently he could hear them. Yet bemusement lurked underneath the tough exterior, a softening that hadn't been present earlier.

"Yes sir," Drake called to the back. Then quieter, "At least I'm earning my pay. And I don't even have to act." He gave her a peck on the lips. "Let's get started, boss."

She responded with her own kiss. "Okay."

He merely laughed.

The morning passed surprisingly well, both in pastry production and family fooling. The mishaps were few and their performance convincing, and she even managed to angle the mirrored mixing bowl just right to get a tantalizing view of Drake's delectable backside without him noticing. She even dared optimism.

Naturally, that's when everything changed.

It began with a little request. "Drake, can you help me with something?"

127

Cynthia approached with a wide smile and a self-assured gait, false innocence defined. Kaitlyn's senses sharpened, even as Drake remained calm and confident. "Sure thing, ma'am." He lowered the bowl of peach frosting and wiped his hands on the back of his jeans. As he passed Kaitlyn, he murmured, "If you don't mind taking a break from watching my ass in the mixing bowl."

She opened her mouth, closed it. Considered feigning innocence. Decided, why bother? "For your information, I do mind," she hissed.

"My cousin said you were a master with the appliances," Cynthia purred, retaking their attention. "I need your expertise."

Uh-oh. During one of their phone calls, she had claimed Drake was a big asset with the kitchen equipment. Yet no matter his skill as an actor, he couldn't operate the complicated professional grade machinery. She had to find a way to distract her cousin. "I thought you were cleaning out the freezer."

"Craig is doing that now. He offered to switch with me."

Yeah, right. Most likely Cynthia badgered her brother until he finally agreed to trade jobs. "Allison is in there. She knows how to work the equipment," Kaitlyn tried again.

"But not fix them," Cynthia countered. "Something is wrong with the kneading machine. It keeps making a loud clunking noise."

Kaitlyn wiped her flour-laden hands on her apron. "I'll take a look at it."

"Is there some reason Drake can't do it?"

The words were a challenge, a thrown gauntlet implying more than they asked. Cynthia was on to them, or at least suspicious. If Drake refused the request, it would ignite the spark of a case she had against them.

"I'd be happy to help." Drake stepped forward, giving

Kaitlyn a slight nod. They silently made their way through the kitchen, Cynthia's expression triumphant, Drake's flush with determination.

As they arrived at the kneader where the rest of the family already stood, Kaitlyn leaned close to Drake. "The townsfolk are here to witness the execution."

He rubbed his hands together. "The jury is still out on this one, sweetheart. Now what seems to be the problem?" He kneeled in front of the silver machine just as it emitted a loud clunking noise, its metal hands jerking back and forth instead of rotating smoothly. He opened several compartments, yet no malfunctions were obvious. Kaitlyn cocked her head to the side. The sound was unusual, almost as if….

"Something is stuck in the motor," she breathed.

"Just what I thought," Drake replied smoothly.

"Here." She grasped his hand and placed it over the opening to the motor compartment. A spark of electricity seemingly passed between them, and for a moment, they just stared at each other. His eyes darkened, their depths filled with gold specks and fathomless emotion.

"I've never seen a couple so mesmerized." Allison's words returned her to the present. Her best friend stared at her with a peculiar expression, strange since she knew about the ruse. Clearly, their acting was convincing.

"That's what happens when you care strongly for each other." Drake spoke with quiet sincerity, almost as if he actually meant it.

No. Kaitlyn exhaled slowly. The line between performance and reality was diminishing like the blazing sun in a twilight sky, but it didn't – couldn't – mean anything. His endearments may seem real, but they beckoned true danger. Danger because it wasn't supposed to be real and danger for the miniscule chance that it was.

She had to focus. With jerky movements, she snapped

opened the motor compartment. "What in the world?" Her focus left Drake for a moment as she reached into the device and removed a smooth pebble. "I think I found the problem," she said dryly, turning to Cynthia. Her cousin boldly returned the gaze, her expression betraying neither guilt nor innocence. It didn't matter. No one else would have sabotaged the machine.

Drake grasped the stone. "A child's prank. One of the kids must've run back here while no one was looking and put the stone in." He didn't mention how careful they were, or how they never would've allowed a child entrance into a kitchen full of dangerous equipment. "There's no time to discuss it. Back to the pastries."

Kaitlyn glared at Cynthia as accusations demanded attention, but Drake's gentle pressure restrained her. She allowed herself to be led from the room, waiting until they were out of hearing range before pivoting to Drake. "She set us up!"

"I know."

"Can you believe her?" She paced back and forth, hissing anger-fueled words, "She could've broken a machine worth thousands of dollars. All to prove me wrong!"

"I know you're upset." He touched her shoulder. "But we must focus if we're going to finish in time."

How could she worry about cookies and croissants when her cousin had tried to sabotage her business? Yet, he was right – if she didn't calm down, she would sabotage it herself.

"Maybe I can distract you."

She looked up sharply. "How are you going to–"

He took her lips.

Fire and passion intertwined in a storm of desire, engulfing her in the power that was Drake Alexander. Instincts blazed, as every part of his body pressed against her. He was hardness defined, muscular and powerful and oh-so-tempting. He caressed her with bold strokes, massaging her neck, her back, then lower, every touch swirling irresistible sensation.

"Drake, we can't do this. Someone will see us." Yet the words were breathless, the tone half-hearted, as she clutched him closer. She couldn't hide the desire mirrored in his eyes.

"Don't we want someone to see us?" He rendered tiny kisses on her neck, branding her with every one, stealing her breath and her willpower to resist. "This is how people who are dating act." He nipped her neck. "They probably won't see us."

It was true. They were all busy with their own tasks, and even Cynthia was likely to stay away for a few minutes after her antics. Yet if he understood that, why was he doing this? "Then why are we..."

"Because of this," he answered the question she didn't finish, returning to her lips, searing them with passion. She splayed her hands on his chest, smoothing the rock-hard expanse. He replicated the motion, caressing her with firm circles, as she delved closer to the powerful man. She could stop, should stop, but even her strength had its limits.

Yet a soft chime sounded, its melodic tone giving Kaitlyn the willpower to pull back. They stood forehead to forehead, nothing separating them, shuddering breaths proving neither possessed complete control. "You're ringing," she breathed softly.

Drake's hesitated, before retrieving a flashing cell phone. For a moment, he studied the screen, before answering the phone quietly, asking the caller to hold. Edging away, she forced her breathing to slow, attempting to calm her furiously beating heart. Disappointment, relief and frustration tangled as his eyes shuttered. "I'm sorry, I have to take this call." Without another word, he pivoted away from her, then banged through the door leading to the parking lot.

What just happened?

The reaction was as mysterious as it was unexpected. Who had inspired such a strong reaction? Family, a friend, a *lover*? What – or who – was he keeping so mysteriously hidden? If only she could hear his conversation…

"Have I descended so far as to consider eavesdropping?" She grabbed a bag of pearlescent icing and started furiously frosting cupcakes. After four attempts at roses that resembled flying saucers, she gave up. "You know what? The answer is yes, I would consider eavesdropping. In fact, I'll do more than consider. He's on my time anyways." She stepped towards the exit, stopped as her dad and Cynthia walked in.

Reluctantly, she addressed Cynthia. "Is the machine acting up again? Did you check for rocks?"

"The machine is fine," her dad broke in with a smile. "I'm just going to the car to get my glasses."

He strolled by, but Cynthia stopped in front of Kaitlyn. "I came to talk to you, my dear," she said in a lilting voice. "It's about Drake. I don't want to put you on the spot, but I'm curious about a few things. Would you mind filling me in?"

Kaitlyn bit back a grimace. How could she refuse without further arousing Cynthia's suspicions? She gave a curt nod, fortifying herself for her cousin's interrogation. Hopefully, Drake was having better luck, whomever he was talking to.

"I TOLD you to only call in an emergency," Cameron spoke in a controlled whisper, only half-successful at keeping the accusation out of his voice. He strove to keep a respectful work environment with his employees, yet it was hard to keep control when the call risked everything. He hadn't missed the suspicion in Kaitlyn's eyes. His all-too-clever employer could have her head plastered against the door. "Is everything all right?"

After his executive vice president spoke, it clearly was an

emergency, at least a business one. One of their most crucial cases had suffered complications, and only he had the knowledge to carve a path forward. He apologized for his earlier brusqueness and gave instructions. After a few minutes of discussion, he finally ended the call and returned the phone to his pocket. He breathed deeply, peered out at the endless blue sky.

What had become of the shrewd businessman, the man who drove through a fierce storm just to make Monday morning's business briefings? He had almost ignored the phone call, a move that would have cost the firm tens of thousands of dollars. Yet if it happened again, he couldn't be certain he could tear himself away from Kaitlyn. "What has she done to you, Cameron?" he whispered out loud.

"That's exactly what I would like to know."

Time stood still.

As a man appeared before him.

And every option disappeared in an instant.

A solemn George Owens stepped forward, his expression as severe as a murder trial. The older man's intelligent eyes pierced him. "Who are you?"

"Mr. Owens…"

"Don't try it, son. I might not be as young or suave as you, but I'm nobody's fool. From the moment I got here, something seemed off, and I heard enough of your conversation to realize you're not some assistant in a candy shop. So either you explain, or I'll get Kaitlyn and we discuss it together."

"Sir, you don't want to do that." If Kaitlyn found out the truth from her father, she would be furious, her reaction unpredictable. He'd have to share the truth soon, that was becoming clearer by the moment, yet he would wait for Cynthia to leave, to not shatter the plan they'd worked so hard to craft.

"You have some explaining to do, son." The words

brought Cameron out of his reverie, and like the businessman he was, he evaluated his remaining choices in seconds. More lies would exacerbate the situation, yet if he told the truth, either the man would kill him or run to Kaitlyn and instruct her to kill him. Neither scenario seemed particularly attractive. Unless he could somehow get the older man to play along...

"I'm waiting." Time was out. As a world class lawyer, Cameron was accustomed to analyzing the probabilities of his success. With one of the most difficult – and vital – choices of his life, in the end he went with his gut.

It was time to tell the truth.

"Kaitlyn and I aren't really together. She hired me to pretend to be her boyfriend to fool Cynthia." Cameron met Mr. Owens' shocked gaze. "Years ago, she told her cousin she was in a relationship, and when Cynthia decided to visit, she couldn't bring herself to admit the truth. Instead, she hired me."

"You're a professional actor?" Mr. Owens choked out. "You're just pretending to be dating?"

"Yes... no... not quite." Cameron exhaled, as images of their *quite* real relationship flashed. How to explain what even he didn't understand.

The older man speared him with a forceful gaze. "What do you mean, not quite?"

Cameron had only one chance to influence the jury, and it had to be the performance of a lifetime. With a deep breath, he began, "My real name is Cameron Drake. I'm a..."

"Big wig from Miami. I thought I recognized you." Mr. Owens folded his arms. "You're somewhat of a celebrity, aren't you? Which makes it all the more confusing – and alarming – you're pretending to be Kaitlyn's assistant."

"I know how it sounds." Cameron chose his words carefully. "I never meant to harm Kaitlyn. In fact, how I feel about your daughter..." He halted, breathed deeply. "I should start from the beginning. On the night of the storm..."

He meant to tell the truth, but he hadn't intended to tell the tale in such detail. With the exception of their intimacy, he shared the entire saga from the moment he arrived until now. Explaining his motives had been difficult, since he didn't exactly understand them, thus he spoke by pure instinct. When he finished, the elder man's expression had softened, however his intentions remained unclear.

This was going to be the difficult part. Cameron stood tall. "I don't want you to tell Kaitlyn."

The older man said nothing for a moment. Then he sighed softly. "You have to tell her."

"I know." Cameron gave a curt shake of his head. "I plan to. I was just hoping to wait until Cynthia left, to save Kaitlyn years of embarrassment and snide comments."

"Unfortunately, I am well-acquainted with my niece's antics." Mr. Owens grimaced. "Believe it or not, I'm actually considering keeping your secret, at least for a little while. But first you have to answer two questions."

Relief soared, of a breadth Cameron hadn't expected. He nodded broadly. "What do you want to know?"

"When did you fall in love with my daughter?"

Cameron froze, as the words reverberated, piercing denials and forging uncertainties. He couldn't love a woman he just met. It was ridiculous. It was mind-boggling. And yet...

He did.

Cameron opened his mouth to deny the accusation, yet the words would not come. Because... any denial would simply be untrue. He loved so much about her – her fire, her spirit, her cleverness, her kindness. *Everything.*

"I don't know," he admitted softly, amidst memories of his

first interaction with the strong-willed woman he now called boss. "But I believe it was the moment we met."

His approval evident, Mr. Owens nodded. "My second question is, how serious are you?"

Cameron didn't have to ask what he meant. Was he planning to stay or go – was this a short-term fling or a long-term commitment? Either decision would alter his life. He could return to his world of wealth and power and live life as if nothing had happened, but that would mean never seeing Kaitlyn again. That simply wasn't an option, not even if building a life with the sweet candymaker meant turning his current world upside down.

She was *everything*.

But he didn't have to give up everything. He'd been considering opening another office for several years, and although Greenfield was small, they were not beyond a long commute to Florida's larger cities. He could base himself here, since much of his work was remote anyways, and go into the office and courtroom when necessary. No matter what, he couldn't lose Kaitlyn.

He wouldn't.

With a deep breath, he gave his reply, "I couldn't be more serious."

"Good man!" Mr. Owens gave Cameron a hearty pat on the back, his exuberance as unexpected as his wide smile. "It's about time my little girl finally met her match. Now don't get me wrong, I don't appreciate the way you've been lying to us and her, but I understand the spirit of the ruse. For years, my wife and I have been hoping Kaitlyn would settle on a real man, and it's finally happened."

Cameron stared at his sudden ally. "There's just one problem. How are we going to convince Kaitlyn to give me a chance when she finds out who I really am?"

Mr. Owens' eyes lit up. "Well, son, you said you were serious about this. You mean that?"

Cameron did not hesitate. "Absolutely."

"You're going to get the chance to prove it. Now listen closely, because I have a plan. Kaitlyn won't stand a chance."

It was time for the closing arguments.

CHAPTER 10

"*N*o, Cynthia, I have no idea if Drake was ever a model, and furthermore I do not care."

Frustration and annoyance tangled as Kaitlyn peered at the door for any sign of the actor or her father. They had left minutes ago, and she only just realized her father might overhear Drake talking on the phone. One wrong sentence, one careless word, and the entire show would be over. Cynthia would be overjoyed, her family disappointed and Drake would...

Leave.

Of course, he would leave eventually no matter what happened. He was only here temporarily and would soon play another part. Why did the thought seem so very painful, almost unacceptable? Was there another way?

What would he do if she asked him to stay?

The door opened, and relief lightened her chest as the two men walked in without any signs of a disagreement, argument or sword fight. Instead, they were talking and laughing in friendly strides, far from the chilled reception of earlier. Kaitlyn strolled to Drake, sliding directly into his outstretched arms. "Everything okay, honey?"

He nodded. "Everything is great."

He seemed sincere, if a little distracted. Had something happened? She couldn't ask with her father standing there, grinning like he'd just caught the goose with the golden eggs. "Great then. Ready to get back to work?"

"Absolutely." Drake wrapped his arms around her, enveloping her in warmth and comfort. Cynthia sniffed haughtily, then strode out of the room without another word. Kaitlyn's father followed with a warm smile.

Drake grimaced. "Not even attempting civility anymore, is she?"

She shook her head. "Not in the slightest. At least I managed to stave off the accusations, for now." She smiled, but her humor quickly faded. "What happened out there? I was worried he overheard you."

"If your father discovered the truth, I wouldn't be able to blackmail you into dating me." His smile was only slightly wicked. "You don't think I'd let that happen, do you?"

She frowned, stepped back. "This is purely a business arrangement."

"Can you really claim that after everything that's happened?"

Not even a little. She crossed her arms over her chest and somehow held her ground as he came nearer. Yet as he loomed ever-closer, her willpower fled, captured by the intensity of six feet plus of pure muscle. She would resist him. She was strong and powerful, and… *oh, forget it.* She kissed him.

The world descended into a whirlwind of passion. She may have started it, but now she surrendered to the force that held her, the man who captured her. He was power defined, hardness and strength and pure temptation. His lips were pliant as he stole her breath, pulling her flush against him. Still, it wasn't enough.

Yet the kiss ended as suddenly as it began, as he pulled back, leaving them both heaving gasps of air. Doubts and uncertainties swirled, brandished by pure rightness. Would she ever be able to resist him?

At least he seemed as disconcerted as her. Gripping her sanity, she breathed, "See, all in your imagination."

He laughed. "Sweetheart, do you actually believe that?"

Never. Yet would she admit it? Never. "Now are you going to work like a responsible employee, or should I write you up for insubordination?"

He flashed a crooked smile. "Anything you say, ma'am. I–" He froze, his grin fading as he stared at something behind her. Ever-so-slowly, she pivoted to…

Catastrophe.

Her cousin stood in the open doorway, flanked by her entire family, their expressions a thousand shades of confusion. With triumphant eyes and an evil sneer, Cynthia's victorious expression was clear. What had she heard?

"You wouldn't believe how sound travels in these old homes, my dear," Cynthia sneered. "He's blackmailing you into dating him?"

Kaitlyn closed her eyes, as the cold words stabbed her. Why had they spoken where others could hear them?

"That's preposterous." Drake's voice was loud, clear and powerful. "Obviously, I was joking."

"I don't believe it." Cynthia stepped into the kitchen, her glossy pink pumps echoing on the gleaming tile floor. "I don't think Drake is your boyfriend at all. In fact, I'm sure of it."

"If that's the case, then why are we eloping?"

The world stilled.

Every breath caught...

As Drake's words echoed endlessly through the air.

Eloping? ELOPING?!!? "Come again?" Kaitlyn whispered.

Drake took her hand. "That's right. We were planning to elope, but now that you're here..." He shrugged. "We may as well make it a celebration."

Somehow, Kaitlyn didn't gasp, faint or demand he send a search party for his mind, which clearly left the premises. Of course, she couldn't appear surprised about the wedding – she was, after all, the bride. Everyone else acted like they had announced they were moving to the moon, but there was no turning back now. If a pretend marriage followed by a pretend annulment was the only way to save the ruse, then so be it. Thus, Kaitlyn gave the only possible response, "So are you coming to my wedding?"

But the real question was, was she?

HAD HE ACTUALLY PROPOSED?

No, his impromptu statement couldn't be considered a proposal. That would have included a question and an answer of agreement from the lady in question. No, he'd given a declaration, an announcement, a notice of upcoming events. He had shocked everyone, most of all himself.

Cameron had said it on a whim, doubting they'd believe the one thing that could silence her cousin. Yet among the shock and surprise, disbelief was strikingly absent. They didn't think he'd lie about such a thing. He must have appeared in control, yet inside he'd been reeling. Eloping. It was impossible.

Or was it?

He'd never believed in love at first sight, but then he'd

never met a woman like Kaitlyn. She was sweet and spirited, clever and kind, everything he could ever imagine or desire. She challenged him, and every moment with her was an adventure. Although they'd only known each other a short time, their connection was undeniable.

It was like their souls knew each other.

An elopement. It sounded crazy, and beyond risky, yet those were the decisions that brought him success for so many years. Of course, he could hire a fake officiant, and then Kaitlyn could claim to have an annulment later. Only what if it wasn't pretend?

What if it was real?

He wanted forever with her. Wanted a marriage and a future and all it entailed. Wanted endless conversations, a million smiles and a forever worth of tomorrows. As certain as he'd ever been of anything, he wanted a life with her.

Of course, it wouldn't be legal without a marriage certificate. Yet that could be another way they proved to Cynthia it was real. They could stop by the government office and procure an authentic one. Of course, it wouldn't take effect unless they actually went through with the ceremony.

He would have to tell Kaitlyn, or rather, *ask* her to share the life he envisioned. Yet he would wait until after the ceremony and her cousin departed. He would simply ask the justice of the peace to wait for his confirmation before filing the paperwork. Thus, he wasn't truly marrying her...

But he would.

WAS THIS A DREAM? A hallucination? Kaitlyn stood in front of the mirror, staring at the reflection that couldn't be her. What had begun as an innocent prank had turned into a surreal fantasy world. Now she was in the bridal suite of Greenfield's finest hall, garbed in her grandmother's white wedding gown, about to walk down the aisle with a man she had only known for a few days.

This couldn't be happening.

Everything had progressed swiftly. After a round of congratulations, they had rushed to finish the special order, and just managed to get it to the ecstatic client in time. Then they set out in full wedding planning mode. She figured they'd do it at home, but her mother had called Greenfield's only hall, and it was actually available because of a late cancellation. A nearby restaurant was accommodating the catering for the small wedding, and the local florist had enough wildflowers for half a dozen simple displays, as well as a cascading bouquet of purple orchids for the bride. Her aunt had rushed here with her grandmother's gown, and ta da, a wedding was made!

As for the cost, Drake said he'd take care of it. Kaitlyn still didn't understand how or why, since a fake wedding should definitely be part of her expenses, but he pointed out it wasn't in the original plan. Of course, there were differences between this and a real wedding. Drake hadn't said where he found the officiant, but she assumed he hired an actor to conduct the ceremony. Obviously, it was not legal, even though Drake had insisted on getting a real wedding license to fool Cynthia. The move had been effective, as the suspicion ever-present in her cousin's eyes finally wavered.

Even though Caitlyn knew it was a ruse, it seemed so real. She still wore the dress, was still walking down the aisle and her family was still here.

This couldn't be happening.

So many emotions tangled at the sight of the blushing bride in the mirror, garbed in winter white. A simple yet elegant creation, the gown featured a fitted bodice, crystal embellishments and a silky skirt. A princess neckline and cap sleeves of wispy chiffon accentuated a simple updo of soft curls. Her features glimmered with shimmery makeup.

She should at least enjoy the rare chance to dress up, yet instead ice pierced her heart, shattering dreams she neither understood nor admitted. Emotion so sharp it burned her chest, sadness that made her eyes heavy with tears. A forged wedding presented the perfect solution. Her plan had succeeded.

So why was she so miserable?

And yet deep down she knew why. With her family's leaving, another would go. A man she had come to care for. A man who delighted her, even if she would never admit it.

A man she loved.

She loved Drake. Was *in love* with him. He had come into her life shrouded by secrets, yet she saw the true man beneath the mystery. He was kind and considerate, giving and so very smart. She loved being with him, whether they were talking or going on a hundred mini-dates, and she wanted nothing more than a million more. Yet that was impossible. He was an employee, not really her fiancé. Today they would walk down the aisle.

Tomorrow he would leave.

"It's almost time," her mother called.

She stepped back from the mirror, from the reflection of a would-be bride celebrating a new life. Her imagination conjured a thousand images of a real wedding day. They would say their vows proudly before family and friends, ready to embark upon a lifetime of happiness. He would pledge unconstrained love, and she the same. Then they would leave together and stay together – forever.

She breathed deeply, taking a step toward the aisle and the would-be future it represented. Although the wedding had been planned a day in advance, a fair group of people had amassed in the small hall. Waiting at the end of the aisle was Drake.

She took another step, stopped as a light tune rang. "Lucky that didn't happen five minutes from now," she murmured as she grasped her phone. Only as her finger hovered over the silent button, the name flashed on the screen. She paused. Why was the Actor's Association calling?

Perhaps it was about the officiant Drake hired. He didn't say he secured one from his company, but it made sense. She connected the call. "This is Kaitlyn."

"Good afternoon, Ms. Owens," the woman spoke in a no-nonsense tone. "I'm following up on our service. The Actors Association takes business very seriously, and we were disappointed we couldn't fulfill your needs. Only we were confused after our actor returned to the office. You said he wasn't easy-going, but he said you didn't even talk to him."

A seed of apprehension sparked, simmering confusion in her chest. "What do you mean he returned to the office?"

"He came back after you turned him away." The woman didn't hesitate. "He's already on another job."

"That can't be the same man." More silence, as the apprehension ignited into unmistakable dread. "Even though he didn't meet my specifications, I kept him. Drake Alexander is my actor."

"Who?"

"Drake Alexander," Kaitlyn said slowly. "The actor you sent."

"We do not employ an actor by that name," the woman sniffed. "Leroy was assigned to your case."

This couldn't be happening. Perhaps Drake had a stage name, like some authors had pen names. She described his physical characteristics, yet the woman denied her once more, "We do not have anyone with that description. Leroy is thin and small, mostly bald."

Kaitlyn opened her mouth, but no words came out. Yet her mind raced, as the description pinged a memory, of a man standing outside her door, the morning after the storm. He'd said he was there for her, but Drake had distracted her with a kiss, and then an unlikely excuse.

Only what if the distraction had been for a purpose? What if Drake knew the man was the real actor? As confusion turned to clarity, suspicion to reality, the truth burned with undeniable starkness. Drake was not an actor.

And if he wasn't an actor…

Who was he?

"I'm so sorry. I have to go." Kaitlyn hung up the phone without a word more, as her heart slammed against her chest, stealing the breath from her lungs. She emerged into a packed room, decorated in white chiffon, cut crystal chandeliers and a thousand dreams. Her mother gave the cue, and suddenly she was gliding on a rose petal-covered aisle, scented by lavender and wildflowers, with Canon in D Major playing in the background. She did not hear a single note, however, as one person captured her entire focus, the man who had stolen her heart, the stranger who waited for her at the end of the path.

She did not walk down the aisle. *She ran.* Drake stood under a gardenia-lined canopy, tall, proud and breathtaking in a full tuxedo. In seconds she reached him, as his woodsy scent overtook her, the power of the towering man engulfing her. She stared at him, and he at her, as his smile faded. Like a darkening sky before a storm, his expression transformed from happiness to concern to suspicion. She grasped his arm and pulled.

For a second, he stood fast, but then he followed her lead while the guests watched in astonishment. They burst into the bridal suite, surrounded by mirrored reflections, jacquard plush seating and gleaming silver adornments.

Kaitlyn locked the door behind them, then pivoted. There were a million things she could say, a thousand questions to ask and a hundred accusations he deserved. In the end, a single question emerged, "Who are you?"

He did not ask what she meant. Did not deny the truth that no longer needed to be said. Instead, understanding transformed his features, as he straightened into a man so different than the assistant or even the actor-for-hire he portrayed. It was all the confirmation she needed.

The man she loved was an imposter.

"I can explain."

"Who are you?" She stood taller, glared. "I deserve to know."

Drake – or whoever he was – didn't hesitate. "My name is Cameron Drake. I run a multibillion-dollar law firm in New York, and before this week I hadn't acted since my award-winning second grade performance in Little Red Riding Hood. I'm pretty well known in my field, and even a bit outside of it, which is why so many people recognized me."

Oh. My. Goodness. He was famous? Words were an impossible feat, as he pressed on, "I was driving home from a business trip when the storm made it too dangerous to remain on the road. I needed shelter and saw your shop from the street. When you mistook me for your actor, something compelled me to go along with it, to pretend to be the actor you thought I was."

He glanced away. "I should have told you. There were a hundred times I almost did. Yet the thought of leaving became more and more difficult until I finally realized what my heart had been telling me since the moment we met." He paused, breathed out. A thousand forevers passed. "I love you."

"What?" she breathed. It couldn't be true. This man was a billionaire who led a national juggernaut. He was a celebrity, known around the world. Beyond their differences, they had only met a few days ago. It was impossible.

And yet somehow she believed it.

He loved her. Despite everything that had happened, everything that *was* happening, it was going to be all right. They were going to be all right, because...

She loved him, too.

For so long she had fought it, but she could no longer challenge fate's will. Her love was instinctual, elemental, beyond *substantial*. His identity did not change what she loved about him. He was still a good man, kind, brave and compassionate, the man with whom she had fallen in love. There was only one thing left to say, "I love you, too."

For a moment, Drake – Cameron – did not say anything. In the next, he was moving toward her. She did not think as she jumped into the arms of the man she knew so well, if not his name, the true person. Neither his name nor his profession mattered. It didn't matter how big his bank account was or how many people read about him on the Internet. She loved him.

He grinned like he'd just been granted his greatest wish. "You do?"

Had she spoken out loud? It didn't matter. "Yes, I do." She beamed. "Of could I do. I do, I do, I do!"

He spun her around, and she laughed in delight. "You still have a lot to make up for." She pointed, softening the words with a smile. "I expect to hear all about your life. The truth, this time, with nothing held back."

"I will never keep a secret from you again," he promised. Yet the slightest bit of uncertainty lit his gaze as he slanted it back to the doorway, where the cadence of conversation had reached fever pitch. "It's great you feel that way, since we're about to get married."

Her smile widened, and her imagination soared. "It may

seem outrageous, but I wish we were getting married for real," she admitted.

"Your wish is my command."

Kaitlyn froze. He didn't mean… he couldn't mean… "But the officiant is an actor."

Cameron shook his head.

She gasped. "You mean…"

He nodded.

What had he done? "You were going to marry me without my consent?"

Cameron laughed. "I'm not that deceitful. It's not legal unless we file the official documents, and I wasn't going to do that until I told you, which I had been planning to do right after Cynthia left. But just in case, the officiant is certified to perform wedding ceremonies." His expression turned serious. "Before we get married, I have something to ask you."

He bent down on one knee.

She gasped as he removed a tiny velvet box from his pocket, opening it to reveal a stunning ring that shimmered like a star. Set in gleaming platinum, it featured a round diamond of at least three carats, surrounded by a halo of tiny stones. In its depths, a thousand fiery rainbows reflected.

"Kaitlyn, I love you more than I ever thought possible. You captured me the moment we met, entrancing me with your spirit, kindness and inner beauty. We've been together days, yet it feels like a lifetime, and I want a lifetime more – and beyond. This is me, Cameron Drake, and I am asking the most important question of my life. Will you be my wife?"

A wave of joy brought watery happiness to her eyes. She grasped Cameron's hands and lifted him up. "Yes," she whispered.

Drake placed the ring on her finger, where it fit perfectly. Then her gorgeous actor… employee… lawyer… boyfriend…

fiancé… *true love* held out his arm. "My dear, are you ready to get married?"

Kaitlyn smiled pure joy as he captured her in his embrace. Then together they journeyed down the aisle and said their vows in what was no performance.

And from that moment on, they never stopped smiling.

Mother

"*M*om, there's something I need to tell you about my husband."

"He's not really your assistant."

Kaitlyn froze, and her next words caught in her throat. After a rather unfortunate impression of a fish, she choked out, "You knew?"

Her mother shrugged. "Of course."

"But... but how?"

"I'm your mother, aren't I?" Her mother winked. "Moms are pretty perceptive when it comes to their daughters."

That made sense, but still... "There's more. We haven't known each other for a long time. We've actually only known each other for a few..."

"Days?"

Kaitlyn blinked. "I'm sorry?"

"Or is it weeks? But it doesn't seem like weeks. My money is on days."

How was this happening? "Did Dad tell you?"

"Oh no," Her mother chuckled. "But it wasn't hard to realize when he figured it out."

This was not going as she imagined. "What else do you know?"

Her mother tapped her chin. "Well, he obviously isn't your personal assistant. I figured he was a friend, or an acquaintance, but you didn't seem to know each other at all. Then I assumed you secured him for the sole purpose of tricking us. Only that still didn't make sense because we weren't supposed to come. However, Cynthia was." She pointed a slender finger. "It seems as if you wanted him there so you could pretend he was your boyfriend and fool Cynthia. Is that about right?"

"Unbelievably so," Kaitlyn said weakly.

"Yet something unexpected happened." Her mother smiled softly. "You didn't intend to fall in love, did you?"

Kaitlyn sighed. "Not even a little."

"So my question is–" Her mother leaned forward. "Was the wedding real?"

Kaitlyn softened at the hopeful look in her mother's eyes. "Yes, it was." Her mother whooped for joy, and she laughed. "It wasn't supposed to be, but in the end, I simply couldn't resist. Believe it or not, there's actually far more to this story."

"Oh, really?" Her mother teased, but soon her expression turned serious. "You know you can tell me anything, sweetie. I love you, and I am always here for you."

Yes, she was. She should have been honest with her mother from the beginning. From now on, she would. "I love you, mom."

Her mother hugged her tightly, like she used to do when she was a little girl. And the world was just a little brighter.

"Do you want to hear the rest?"

"I can't wait."

"Would you believe he's a billionaire lawyer who is also a celebrity?"

Her mother stared for a moment, before her smile widened. "Absolutely."

Brothers

"I'M GOING to teach him a lesson."

"No." Kaitlyn grabbed her brother's arm. "We were both involved in the deception."

"But he fooled you first, which is unacceptable. No one takes advantage of my little sister."

"You can't be serious. What are you going to do? Punch him?"

"Sounds like a plan to me." Jesse grinned.

"What? No," Craig denied. "I was going to threaten to sue him."

She looked upwards. "You don't want to do that. He runs a multibillion-dollar law firm."

"I suppose I'll just have to punch him."

"Jesse!"

"Just kidding, sis." Her brothers grinned, boasting twin mischievous gleams. "But is it all right if we make him think we will?"

"No!"

Her gigantic brothers pouted, grumbling about not having any fun. Their expressions sobered a moment later. "Are you certain you're all right?" Craig asked softly. "He didn't pressure you into marrying him, did he?"

"Of course not," she confirmed. "He asked." She wouldn't mention he planned the wedding ceremony first, or that he may not have given up. He was a man accustomed to getting what he wanted. Thankfully, they both wanted the exact same thing – each other.

"As long as you're happy." Jesse gave her a hug. "But next time, be honest with us. We're your brothers, and we always have your back."

Yes, they did. They truly were wonderful men. When they opened their arms. she gave them the biggest hug ever.

And they all grinned.

Cynthia

"Cynthia, there's something I need to tell you about Drake, something I've been keeping from you for a long time."

"I knew it!" Beady eyes sparkled with triumph. "What is it? Are you guys not actually married? Is he a convict? Is he cheating on you? Whatever it is, just admit it."

"Well..." Kaitlyn whispered, leaning forward." The truth is..." She leaned closer. "He's actually a..." Closer still. "Billionaire lawyer who runs his own national law firm."

And for once...

Cynthia was speechless.

Cameron (one year later)

"I've been keeping something from you."

"I suspected as much." The powerful man placed a hand under her chin. "I thought we were done with secrets."

"Since you kept such a big one, don't I get a turn?"

"That's not how it works," he murmured. "When you keep secrets, there are consequences."

A chill traced down Kaitlyn's spine. She shivered, leaning back against the sateen sheets of her – their – bed. If she delved any closer, she would get caught in the power that was Cameron Drake, and they had far too important matters to discuss right now.

She breathed air scented with gardenias, spice and heady male. They were in the luxurious master bedroom of their new home, built right next to the candy shop. Actually, it was more a mansion, which Cameron had designed. At least she could now dedicate the entire other building to her business. Although…

It was not the only location of her business. With Cameron's support, she'd opened two bakeries in neighboring towns. She chose locations that did not have similar establishments, welcoming communities eager for new business. Thus far the ventures had proven extraordinarily successful. They provided fresh culinary delights, employment opportunities and lots of charity events, such as free candy-making parties for disadvantaged children.

Cameron had continued with his own business, of course, being a lawyer, not an actor. He built a satellite office nearby and commuted to the city several times a week. He'd become even more famous, as all the news stations picked up on his move, especially when his billionaire buddies stopped by. Life was hectic but wonderful, as they recreated every one of their miniature dates in full splendor. Their love blossomed, in a life that was truly an adventure.

Yet now it was time for a new adventure.

Cameron leaned closer, dipping the bed under his

formidable size. He was still fully dressed in his suit, while she wore only a silky nightgown. He traced a finger down her neck. "Someone has been hiding." He explored further, trailing between her breasts. "Don't tell me it's another actor."

"Oh no." She shuddered as he made lazy circles on her stomach, then delved *lower*. "It's someone far smaller. In fact so small, you can't really see him – or her – yet."

He stilled.

Stared.

"What?" he breathed.

"The little one is too small to see." Now she moved to explore him, smoothing hard muscle. "However, you'll meet him or her in about seven months."

His gaze tracked down. "You don't mean you're...."

"Yes."

Elation sparkled, as bright as the stars twinkling outside their window. She matched his smile, allowing all the joy and love to flow through her. For him, her and the little one who would soon expand their family. "Are you happy?"

"There are no words." He touched her belly reverently, with wonder, delight, and pure, unadulterated love. "I love you," he whispered to the little one, before lifting his gaze. "And I love you."

"Forever," she whispered.

"And ever," he promised.

And forever it was.

BONUS EPILOGUE

"*Y*ou were right." Cameron toasted his friends with a glass of thousand-dollar-a-bottle brandy. "Life as a married man is an adventure. And–" He grinned. "The best thing in the world."

Knowing expressions greeted him, from the group the press had dubbed The Billionaires of Miami. They hailed from different backgrounds, leaders of various industries, yet they were all extraordinary. The world couldn't get enough of the wealthy, powerful men.

"Goodness, you are besotted." Royce lifted his own glass. "Yet I can't say I blame you. I feel the same about Elora."

That Royce was madly in love with his wife was obvious. Few would believe they married before they actually met, a secret they held for many months. When they finally came face to face, Elora was pretending to be someone else. Now they were nearly inseparable. "How is Elora and the little one?" Cameron asked.

Royce's eyes lit up, as they always did when he spoke of his family. "Wonderful. We've just started another foundation."

Cameron and the others bestowed well wishes and congratulations. Every man here contributed millions to charity, through countless organizations and initiatives. Of course, Cameron fought for charitable causes in his law practice, with a division that took on crucial work pro bono. Others helped in different ways, such as Dominick, who wielded the power of the pen.

He turned to the entrepreneur/author, "When is your new book coming out?"

"Next week." Dominick nodded. "It's poised to hit number one on the lists."

Cameron didn't doubt it. His friend's first book had been a runaway bestseller, giving the head of the massive computer conglomerate instant fame. He had gotten a break from that fame when he went undercover at his own company to investigate suspected corruption. He met his future wife during that time, who had no idea the man she fell in love with was actually the billionaire CEO of the company.

"Congratulations." Cameron clapped him on the shoulder. "You must be thrilled."

"I am," Dominick rumbled. "Mostly because the proceeds are going to mental health charities."

"Good news all around." Cameron lifted his glass again, as did the other men, and yet one lifted his a little less, Aidan Bancroft was atypically solemn, his expression tight and constrained. "You all right, buddy?"

Aidan's gaze snapped up. "Yes, of course."

Yet the words rang false, to the others clearly, as each lowered their glass. "Is there anything we can do for you?" Cameron asked quietly. "We're here for you, with anything you need."

It was true. They were more brothers than friends,

providing support and kinship. They would always be there for each other, yet Aidan was fiercely private.

Thus, it was an utter shock when he stated flatly, "A woman claimed to have my child."

That Cameron didn't show astonishment was a testament to his restraint. The others showed varying levels of surprise, no doubt regarding the accusation itself, and not any belief it could be true. They knew Aidan well. If he fathered a child, he would take responsibility.

"Of course, I would never allow my child to grow up without a father." Aidan hardened. "If something happened, I would take immediate responsibility and provide extensive support. More than anything, I would be involved in his or her life. Of course, the child cannot be mine."

"We have no doubt." Cameron nodded. "What did she say when you confronted her?"

"That was the strange part. She retreated immediately and seemed overly eager to leave. It's even stranger since she was a reporter."

A dozen grimaces responded. They were all incessantly hunted by the media. "Was she doing a story?"

"At first, I thought so." Aidan looked straight ahead, his eyes unfocused. "Yet now I'm not so sure. I must do some investigating." He rubbed his hands together. "I will find out everything I can about her and her story. She deceived the wrong man."

Cameron smiled at the determination, and challenge, in the man's voice. He almost pitied the poor reporter. She would soon learn the consequences of her actions.

"Enough about me. This one is all about you." Aidan raised his drink high this time. "To your happy ending."

"To your happy ending," the men echoed.

And it was, indeed, a happy ending.

THE BILLIONAIRE'S SECRET CHILD

*T*hank you for reading Undercover Billionaire. I hope you enjoyed my characters and world. My next book, The Billionaire's Secret Child, will be FREE in Kindle Unlimited.

Chapter 1

IT WAS the type of house you pointed at as you drove past in your squeaky, middle-aged sedan. The one that made you gasp – just a little – as you stared in dreamy wonder at its soaring stories, expansive lawns and pristine gardens. The home you'd never own, no matter how many extra hours you put in at the office or how many promotions you scored. The one your boss couldn't afford, nor his boss and probably not even the one above him.

It made you wonder who could afford it. If you knew this person to be a business tycoon and a self-made billionaire, as was the case with this particular man, then you automatically knew aspects of his personality: Strong. Powerful. Intelligent. In control. Yes, indeed, Aidan Bancroft was all of these. Plus, one other moniker, which even he didn't know:

Father.

Laura Blake's heart slammed against her ribs, stealing the oxygen from her lungs, as she pulled into the engraved stone driveway. Close up, the house loomed even larger, powerful and massive, just like its owner. Three stories tall and quadruple the width, the building seemed better suited for a dozen families than a single man. White surfaces gleamed in the slanting sun, with rounded pillars, majestic turrets and lush, manicured lawns stretching for acres. Ten, twenty, thirty, who knew how many rooms the mansion had? Yet she could not let the size of the home intimidate her from dealing with the man inside. For her child, she would engage with anyone, no matter how ruthless. Of course, Aidan Bancroft wasn't just ruthless.

He was a famous, powerful billionaire businessman. A man who got what he wanted – whatever it was.

Laura stopped at a huge white gate, its bars etching a majestic lion, a fitting symbol for the authoritative man. Four security cameras recorded her every move (How many were hidden?) as she cranked down her window to expose the brass intercom system. Silencing the instincts urging her to flee before it was too late, she reached out and pushed the button on the intricate device.

"May I help you?" A professional female voice spoke crisply through the air.

"I'm here to see Mr. Bancroft." Laura fought to keep her voice emotionless, her tone even, yet an edge belied her efforts. *Stay strong.*

"Do you have an appointment, ma'am?"

"No." Laura exhaled slowly, refused to even consider failure. Straightening, she launched into the speech she'd planned, one that would hopefully pique their curiosity enough to allow her entrance. "I represent someone very close to Mr. Bancroft, a person who lost touch with him. Seeing him could literally mean life or death. It will only take a moment."

The first two assertions were true, the last an optimistic gambit. Hopefully, the woman wouldn't ask for details.

"Ma'am, are you a reporter?"

Laura closed her eyes at the question she'd hoped they wouldn't ask. For although her job had no relation to her visit, she was indeed a reporter. And everyone knew the reclusive Mr. Bancroft spoke to very few reporters.

"No," she lied, since an affirmative would shatter any chance of admittance. Her daughter's future bore more weight than total honesty. And, in this case, she didn't play the role of reporter.

"Your name, ma'am?"

"Laura Blake." He would not recognize the name, should never even know she existed. Of course, everyone knew him: Aidan Bancroft, billionaire founder and CEO of Bancroft Enterprises, an international conglomerate with dealings in dozens of industries. Unlike many men who ran such companies, Aidan Bancroft was in the prime of his life, gorgeous with the body of a movie star. The combination of good looks, charm and power had propelled him to super-stardom, as well as the cover of half the business and popular magazines and every social media site. He hobnobbed with television stars, presidents and royalty, with practically every single woman on the planet (and probably some on neighboring planets) hoping to become Mrs. Bancroft.

Likely, they would assume she was here to give a proposal, decent or indecent. They would ask more questions, or just refuse her outright. Thus, she started in shock when a low buzzing sounded, and the gate began to open. "Drive through," the voice commanded, then clicked off.

Could it truly be this easy?

Not likely.

Yet she did not hesitate, as she shifted the car into gear and slowly pulled through the gate. From up close, the home was even more impressive, a storybook palace come to life. Emerald green vines and lavender flowers twined around its gleaming sides, framing stained glass windows with rich brocade curtains and intricate crown molding. Curved walls sketched whimsical features, an architectural delight that rose like a masterpiece against the cerulean sky. The scent of gardenias drifted through the air, as birds sang their melodies, darting between the densely flowered bushes.

At any other time, she would have stopped, taken minutes or hours to stare in awe, but now she noted the beauty only briefly, as she glided to the challenge ahead. She parked next to a gleaming new Porsche, which was next to a gleaming new Jaguar, which was next to a gleaming new Ferrari, which was next to something that looked like it could probably fly. Fortifying herself for the inevitable, she exited the car and strode to the front of the house. She stood straight in front of the two giant oak doors and rang the bell.

Undoubtedly, she would be greeted by a secretary or assistant, someone who would ask questions, examine her intentions and then turn her away (with or without laughter, teasing and/or pity). Just because she gained admittance to the grounds didn't mean she would actually see the master of the domain. Thus, when none other than the infamous Aidan Bancroft himself, international business mogul, America's top bachelor and *father of her child*, opened the door, the world froze.

Or at least she did. She had seen pictures, read about him on the Internet, heard countless stories, but nothing could have prepared her for the actual man, flesh, blood and a whole lot of *muscle*.

He was gorgeous – no, not merely gorgeous – stunning. With thick brown hair and sea blue eyes, he boasted a model's face, chiseled and flawless, perfection defined. He towered to well over six feet, with a muscular build that cast him above the average man and far beyond Laura's petite stature. Hidden strength loomed beneath the crisp three-piece suit, power present yet controlled. He drew her in, for more reasons than his appearance. Whereas in the photographs this strength had been apparent, now it was all but overwhelming. No wonder millions fawned over him, hoping for a small piece of him.

A piece she had.

Laura met his gaze. Awareness shot through her, electrifying already over-stimulated senses. Her skin tingled as pinprick goose bumps formed, as he held her captive in a gaze as secure as iron shackles. Her shallow breathing sounded as loud as a raging river; her rapidly beating heart thundered like an erupting volcano. A mixture of cologne and sandalwood assailed her, intoxicating her senses and capturing her attention. And suddenly, an altogether shocking sensation assailed her.

Attraction.

Fighting for focus, Laura pushed aside the traitorous feelings. Of course, he attracted her like a gourmet cupcake (the type with freshly whipped cream and drizzled chocolate) – he would affect any sane woman – but that couldn't play a part in her mission. Her daughter was all that mattered. She needed something much simpler and far more important than unbidden lust.

"Mr. Bancroft, I assume."

The man nodded, but made no comment. He neither welcomed her to his home nor invited her in. After a moment's hesitation, she continued. She would not be intimidated.

"I need something from you." She stood tall. "I was hoping you could spare a moment for a few simple questions."

"I'm sure you are." When he finally spoke, his deep baritone held not the slightest bit of warmth. "I'm certain you have many questions. You are, after all, a reporter."

Her breath caught in her throat. How had he found out so quickly?

"Surprised I know?" He studied her as if he could discern her every secret. "Paparazzi stalk me on a daily basis, with outrageous stunts worthy of reality show television. Did you think I bought your story about a long-lost relation? Don't you think I would have asked for this fictional relation's name if I thought it were true?" Furious eyes flashed. "The only reason you're here is so I can tell you that you have no chance of infiltrating my business. I have ways to investigate – and control – uninvited visitors. As I'm sure you're aware of, Ms. Blake, I do not see reporters, and I do not care for liars, so have a nice trip back to Greenfield."

The man moved to close the door. "Wait!" Laura shot her hand inside the portal. He glared, but she couldn't let it end here. She might never get another chance to make her case.

"Mr. Bancroft, it's not what you think. You have to listen to me," she implored.

The man widened the door ever so slightly. "If it's not what I think, then tell me what it is," he responded quietly.

In a moment's span, every option flashed, every path and every decision. Yet only one seemed to have any possibility, infinitely small, of gaining his cooperation. She would have to reveal the *truth*.

The moment she had been anticipating for five long years had finally come.

"I ask you again, do you contest that, madam? Do you

deny you're a reporter?" A strong voice snapped Laura back to the present, back to the gargantuan mansion, the handsome boardroom warrior. Slowly, she shook her head.

"Then we've wasted enough of each other's time. Goodbye." Again, he went to close the door, but again she stopped him. This time, however, it was not with an action but with words.

"Do you remember the Peace Fields Fertility Clinic?" Her breath froze, as she awaited the response that could refine her world.

His eyes flashed with rage, and Laura clamped her mouth shut. He was furious, but why? Would he slam the door in her face, banish her and any hope of getting what she'd come for? For a moment, it seemed he would, yet instead he opened the door wide. "Come in," he commanded.

She released a breath. She had definitely not mistaken the man as her daughter's father. The powerful stranger would have exiled her for life if he hadn't recognized the name of the clinic.

"It seems I underestimated you." He looked at her with fathomless eyes. "Follow me."

She walked behind the formidable man, following him through a spectacular hall filled with priceless paintings and antiques. If the exterior of the house had been stunning, the inside was breathtaking, with high sweeping ceilings and elegant gilded fixtures. It was scented with spice and oak, and set to the melody of a two-story waterfall that flowed into a lush indoor rose garden. Gold and marble furnishings adorned large airy rooms, resplendent with ornate furniture and oversized decor.

Laura vaguely remembered the mansion being featured on one of the entertainment shows, but the thought was fleeting. As she walked behind Mr. Bancroft, her quest usurped every thought. That was, until he stopped.

And she ran into him.

For a moment, time halted, the world faded, as attraction swept through her like a tidal wave. She pressed against his powerful body, flush against unparalleled strength. Hard muscles leapt beneath her hands, firing the inexplicable urge to get closer. Instead, she jumped back.

"I apologize!" What had come over her? The stress of the situation and the proximity of the handsome man had clearly unbalanced her. A man whose child she had carried in her body.

Something fired in his eyes. It was not anger like earlier, or even distaste. It almost seemed like... interest. But it couldn't be, as he abruptly pivoted and led her to a large living room flanked by thick maroon rugs and large velvet sofas. He gestured for her to take a seat, even as he remained standing. She declined the seat (he already towered above her) as well as the drink an impeccably dressed butler offered. She would need all her faculties to get through this meeting.

Mr. Bancroft removed an object from the drawer of a large marble desk. Surprise and confusion tangled. "What are you doing with a checkbook?"

"How much?"

What? He couldn't actually believe she would use her daughter as a payday. She shook her head firmly. "I don't want your money."

Mr. Bancroft breathed deeply, clearly fighting for control, as he placed the checkbook down on the desk. Likely, the amount would have been substantial, but it didn't matter. She would never blackmail a man for the most precious blessing in her life.

She never thought she would come here at all, approach this man whose fame and wealth rivaled few. But after her father's near-fatal heart attack, his second before sixty, life took on a new meaning. She needed to protect her daughter, even from her own genes, and she could only do that with her father's medical history. The vital information would allow her to prepare for any potential conditions or diseases that ran in the family. She wanted nothing else.

She most certainly didn't want to touch those muscles.

Definitely didn't want to test how hard they were.

And press against them? Out of the question.

"Ms. Blake," Mr. Bancroft growled lowly. The suave businessman was gone, replaced by a predator, dominating pure power. "I don't know what game you're playing, or what you hope to attain. You can drop the innocent act, because we both know you're not here for a friendly chat. However, you do have information I would rather keep out of the papers. I could sue or bully you, however if I did, the secret would undoubtedly emerge. I would rather get this over with, easy and painless."

"Mr. Bancroft, you're mistaken." Laura raised her hands, to stop him or shield herself? "I'm not after your money."

"So that's how it's going to be? Nothing will keep this story out of the papers, no matter its power to shatter my life."

Laura closed her eyes. She had known he didn't want Jeanie, but to claim she shattered his life? She opened her eyes, expecting anger, but something far more powerful lurked in his expression: pain, anguish even. Confusion reigned once more. "I'm not going to put anything in the papers," she said softly, even as his gaze turned incredulous. "I'm not lying."

"Just like you weren't lying when you said you weren't a reporter," he snapped.

"That was different. Listen…"

"No, it's time you listened." He strode to her, blasting a hole through her personal space and her senses. "I've met reporters who employed dirty tricks, but never one who would sink to this level. You're blackmailing me for the most tragic situation of my life."

"Tragic situation of your life?" The world turned blistering red. How dare the man call her beautiful angel a tragedy! "What are you talking about? It's not that big a deal."

Somehow her words infuriated him even more. "Not that big a deal?" he snarled. "First my wife can't have a child, then we go to a fertility clinic to search for a miracle and after that miracle finally happens, she's killed. Somehow you find out and decide to blackmail me. Does that not sound like a big deal to you?"

Oh. My. Goodness.

Her world... her life... reality shattered.

Everything that once made sense, the truths that formed the basis for her life, disappeared, rearranging into an entirely new existence. She knew he had a wife who passed away in a car crash, but not of any child or fertility problems. But still, something was missing. If he was at the clinic to help his wife become pregnant, then why...

"You weren't an anonymous donor," she whispered as everything fell into place, as the pieces of the puzzle locked together to form a horrifying image. The once inexplicable suddenly made sense: his confusion, his anger, his actions. Mentioning the fertility clinic must have opened new wounds of losing the child his wife had carried. But Jeanie was undoubtedly his, the documents proved it, and even more significantly, his features were unmistakable in her little face. Which meant the clinic had made a very large, very consequential mistake.

Fuzzy memories came back at her, memories of news stories about Aidan's wife, Leanne Jo. Laura gasped softly. Leanne Jo Bancroft, LJB, just like Laura Jane Blake. If they used initials to identify the patients...

"Of course, I wasn't an anonymous donor. Any child of mine would know me well," Aidan ground out the words. "Very well."

Laura gaped, her heart racing like the favorite at the Preakness Stakes. And suddenly the consequences multiplied a thousandfold. Before coming, she had affirmed Jeanie's biological father would have no legal rights – no court in the land would contest that. But if the donor had been unwilling? He would definitely have a case, and from the looks of it, he would want it. The ramifications were staggering, the implications life-changing. Would he try to take her daughter away from her? Would he be a good father, or would he hurt Jeanie? She needed time to think, time to grapple with this new information before the powerful man stole her every choice.

"How did you know about the fertility clinic?" Aidan's voice was low, dangerous. "We specifically used a center in the middle of nowhere to keep the press away. My wife's doctor arranged everything. Now, five years later, somehow you find out. Who shared the secret?"

An image of the friendly, young receptionist with corkscrew curls arose. The truth had garnered her cooperation, the explanation that Laura's father had suffered two heart attacks and she needed medical records to ascertain if heart disease ran on the biological father's side as well. Aidan would be appalled to learn who had given away his most precious secret. Of course, the bubbly girl didn't give the information to a stranger, but to the child's mother.

Of course, his anger was justified – he thought she was trying to barter secrecy for money – but it still didn't explain everything. Why was he so desperate to hide his visit to a fertility clinic, even willing to provide a la carte access to his bank account to protect it? She could name no less than half a dozen celebrities who had used such clinics; nowadays it really didn't comprise news. Why did he offer to pay her instead of sending her on her way the moment she mentioned the clinic?

And if he protected such a minor detail like a top secret military operation, what would he do when he discovered the *true* secret?

She couldn't reveal her source, at least not yet. If he visited the clinic, he would discover what they really were to each other. "Someone sent an anonymous e-mail, claiming to possess vital information they would exchange for a reasonable price. He revealed the name of the clinic, saying he heard your wife talking about it to a friend at a coffee shop years ago. That was it."

Aidan looked suspicious, but at least he didn't immediately accuse her of lying to protect his secret child. "Did you get his name?"

She shook her head. "Informants don't typically give names. We only communicated online, and I received no response to my last e-mail. I'm sorry, I can't help you more."

It wasn't the most convincing argument, but hopefully he wouldn't storm the clinic looking for her informant. For now, she had to depart this impossible world of wealth and power, leave his overwhelming presence, so she could consider her next move. She turned to the door, made it two steps.

"How could a single mother do such a thing?"

Laura froze. He wasn't talking about the informant – he was talking about *her*. Somehow, he knew she had a daughter.

Did he know she was his?

"Didn't think I knew, huh?" His heavy boots echoed on the floor as he stalked closer. "My investigators are pretty thorough. In five minutes, they produced quite a bit of information about you and little Jeanie."

Laura fought to form thoughts, to concoct a plan, to *breathe*. One wrong word could shatter her life and her choices. Details like her job and status as a single mom would be easy to find, yet the truth about Jeanie's paternity should be impossible to discover, at least in five minutes.

Yet Aidan Bancroft wielded power like few others.

He didn't give her a chance to respond. "Any mother with a heart shouldn't be capable of what you're doing. How much do you love your child?"

The answer was automatic. "More than my own life."

"Then how can you exploit the loss of mine?" he thundered, fiery emotion blazing. "How could you remind me of what I almost had... what I lost." The last words were but a whisper, pure grief.

The oxygen thinned in the room, awash with a million unshed tears. She had to fight, had to keep chaotic emotions from overwhelming her. His feelings were warranted – he thought she was blackmailing him over a lost child. Only a truly cruel person could exploit such a tragedy, yet was she doing worse by not immediately telling him about Jeanie? Guilt sliced through her, indecision and uncertainty muddying every path. No – she needed to protect her daughter, and that meant waiting to tell him until she had time to consider her new reality. "Mr. Bancroft, I'm so very sorry. I obviously came under false pretenses, and your comments were completely understandable. I'll let myself out." She pivoted towards the door.

She didn't make it far.

A hand brushed across her arm, igniting an electric spark. Sensual awareness rocked her body. "Wait just a moment." His eyes danced with suspicion. "What are you up to?"

Had she imagined he would just let her go? She stared up at a mountain of power. "Nothing. I thought about what you said, and I felt guilty. We reporters do have consciences, you know." She shrugged, feigning cool indifference that could not be further from the truth. "Your story just tugged at mine."

"You're lying again."

Laura nearly stumbled. He grasped her arm with one large hand, easily encircling her as he steadied her. Once more his eyes flashed with *something*. Did he feel the current between them, just below the surface, far beyond the quest? Something indescribable forged a connection, stronger than anything she'd ever before felt.

No. She couldn't succumb to whatever this was. She pulled back, smoothed invisible wrinkles from her inexpensive suit. She should expect perceptiveness from a man who made his first million by the time he reached twenty, his first billion by twenty-five. But now she had to get past it, had to convince him her story was true. "I thought you'd be happy. I'm not going to write any articles, and I'm certainly not going to blackmail you. Please believe me."

Aidan tilted his head back. Slowly, he spoke, "Even if you're telling the truth, I still don't understand. You come in here with a story worth a fortune, and now you're going to walk away? I'm putting two and two together and not coming out with four. Tell me what's going on," he commanded.

Laura shuddered under the man's heavy gaze. At least he wasn't putting one and one together and coming up with three. She fought the urge to tell him everything, to give in to his demands. Although he probably wouldn't believe the truth, what if he did? Likely, he would control everything about her and Jeanie's life from that moment forward. She needed time to ponder her choices before making a move. "There's nothing," she said slowly, "except for what I've already told you. I have to go."

The man in front of her did not move, an insurmountable

obstacle seizing all power. And judging by his solid form, she had no hopes of getting past him should he not wish it. "You're playing with fire." He moved closer, crowding her. "I performed three hostile takeovers from corrupt executives this morning, and that was just business. But this... this is personal."

Laura gulped, tried to move back. He didn't let her. "This isn't a hostile takeover." Her voice emerged a whisper as the man towered above her.

"Is that right?" he drawled with complete control. "Are you certain?"

No. Not really. Not even a little.

Suddenly he relaxed, and his lips rose, forming what could only be called a smile. It created an extraordinary transformation in the man, an astounding change that stole her breath. For the first time, she could see what lay beneath his powerful and cool exterior – the beauty, the wisdom, the power. Soft lines appeared around his eyes, telling her that despite what she had seen today, this was a man who liked to smile. What would it be like if they met in different circumstances?

"I don't know why, but for some reason I believe you won't print my story."

Story? Still dazed from the smile, Laura fought to return to the present. Ah yes, the story he thought she was writing. Relief slipped through the chaos unnerving her mind.

"But–" He held up his finger. "I know there's something more. If it has anything to do with me, I'm going to find out."

THE BILLIONAIRE'S SECRET CHILD, will be FREE in Kindle Unlimited.

· · ·

WOULD YOU LIKE A FREE NOVELLA?

Sign up for my newsletter at www.MelanieKnightAuthor.com and receive The Billionaire's Secret Wife.

The Billionaire's Secret Wife

SHE MARRIED a man she'd never met. Why won't he let her go?

Marry a man she'd never met? Outrageous, ridiculous, *impossible*. Yet to save her nephew, Elora Livingston weds powerful billionaire Royce Livingston, separated by continents in a virtual wedding. The marriage was supposed to be temporary, even as they grow ever-closer through letters and phone calls. She must leave the fantasy, but...

He won't let her go.

Donning a disguise, she infiltrates a glittering charity ball at his lavish mansion, determined to dissolve the marriage once and for all. Yet unexpected desires soar, forging a connection she cannot deny. No one knows the woman in their midst is the powerful man's wife, as one question burns above all:

Does he recognize her?

His wife thinks he married her to gain an inheritance, but Royce Livingston has altogether different motives. He cannot ignore the connection with the alluring woman, built through a thousand stories and endless conversations. As secrets swirl, he fights for the most important merger in his life. He will show her what life is like as...

The Billionaire's Secret Wife.

Books in The Secret Billionaires Series:

Billionaire in Disguise

WHEN ADRIANA RECRUITS her company's newest intern to pretend to be her boyfriend, she has no idea he's actually the billionaire CEO in disguise.

Undercover Billionaire

Kaitlyn hires an actor to be her fake boyfriend, only the powerful man isn't what she ordered. It's a case of mistaken identity, but the billionaire lawyer goes along with the ruse.

The Billionaire's Secret Child

What if you had to tell a man he was a father - not of an unborn life, not of a swaddled infant, but of a child of four? Sound difficult? Then how about this: What if you had to tell a man you never met?

For exclusive news, giveaways and surprises, subscribe to my newsletter at www.MelanieKnightAuthor.com.

I love connecting with readers on social media. **The Secret Crusaders: Melanie's Romance Readers is my Facebook group for everything romance.**

FOLLOW ME ON SOCIAL MEDIA:

Facebook
Tiktok

I also write historical Regency romance under the name
Melanie Rose Clarke. Check out my books, all available now
in Kindle Unlimited.
Escaping the Duke
Captured by the Earl
The Untamed Duke

THE SECRET BILLIONAIRES SERIES

Billionaire in Disguise

Wanted: Fake boyfriend

Qualifications: Must be charming and friendly. No criminal masterminds. Prior experience as a fake boyfriend a plus.

Responsibilities: Convince my large family you are my boyfriend, so I don't ruin their celebration. May involve shirtless jogs, splash fights and lots of practice kissing.

Applicant Name: Dominick Knight, a.k.a. Nick Walters

Employment: Billionaire CEO of Knight Technology, undercover as a temp to investigate corruption.

Special skills: Keeping my true identity a secret.

🌱

Final result: Secrets, seduction and excitement.

Undercover Billionaire

Her: She's sassy, intelligent and strong, and she's had enough of men trying to run her life. Problem is, she needs a man – and quick – to be the non-existent fiancé she's been bragging about to the family. Enter Drake Alexander, hired with the best of credentials from a top-notch acting association. Only he's not exactly what she's ordered...

Him: He's rich, powerful and just a little bit arrogant, and he doesn't need any more women running after his billions. Problem is, he's stuck in the storm of the century in some hole-in-the-wall town. Banging on the door of a local, the last thing he expects is to be greeted by a beautiful woman ranting about how he's the preposterously late actor she's been expecting. Yet for some reason, he lets her believe the lie....

Kaitlyn has no choice but to accept Drake as her pretend fiancé, even though he invades her thoughts and unsettles her life. Worse yet, continues to play his role even when her family is not around! Soon they're planning a pretend wedding, getting closer and closer to "I do." Sparks fire and suspicions soar, but everything changes when...

The truth is revealed.

The Billionaire's Secret Child

What if you had to tell a man he was a father - not of an unborn life, not of a swaddled infant, but of a child of four?

Sound difficult? Then how about this:

What if you had to tell a man you never met?

Reporter Laura Blake always imagined she would have a child the old-fashioned way, but when life didn't work out that way, she conceived her daughter through the wonders of technology. Five years later, life is perfect... until her father's two heart attacks, and a newfound quest emerges: find the man who fathered her child to attain potentially life-saving medical records. Only the anonymous donor is not the stranger she imagined, but Aidan Bancroft, famous billionaire known for attaining what and who he wants. Furthermore...

He never was an anonymous donor.

Aidan is furious when a reporter confronts him with impossible claims. He only visited the fertility clinic to conceive with his late wife, and lost everything. Yet soon it becomes clear there is far more to her story. He will discover everything there is to know about Laura Blake and her child.

Stunned by the news and their life-altering ramifications, Laura flees, hoping for time to carve the future. Yet Aidan follows her, his suspicions forging his own investigation. As passions soar and emotions flourish, they delve closer and closer. Soon Aidan is chasing more than his suspicions.

What happens when the truth is revealed?

ABOUT THE AUTHOR

Melanie Rose Clarke has wanted to be a writer since she was a little girl. Sixteen years ago, she married her own hero, and now she creates compelling stories with strong heroines, powerful males and, of course, happily every afters. She writes historical (regency) romance, contemporary romance, paranormal romance, romantic suspense and women's fiction.

Melanie is a three-time Golden Heart® finalist. Her manuscripts have earned numerous awards in writing competitions, including several first place showings. With over two decades of professional writing experience, Melanie has written thousands of pieces for businesses and individual clients. She has worked in advertising and marketing, and her freelance articles on the web have garnered hundreds of thousands of views.

She writes amidst her five beautiful children, her dream come true. Besides writing, she loves to read, exercise and spend time outdoors. She is a member of Mensa. For more information, visit her website at www. MelanieKnightAuthor.com.

Made in United States
Troutdale, OR
04/08/2025

30439259R00106